CLASSICS
OF
RUSSIAN
LITERATURE

А. ПУШКИН

Повести Белкина

ИЗДАТЕЛЬСТВО ЛИТЕРАТУРЫ НА ИНОСТРАННЫХ ЯЗЫКАХ

МОСКВА

1954

A. PUSHKIN

The Tales of Ivan Belkin

FOREIGN LANGUAGES PUBLISHING HOUSE

MOSCOW

1954

Translated from the Russian
by IVY *and* TATIANA LITVINOV

Illustrated by
D. A. SHMARINOV,
Stalin Prize winner

Designed by
S. M. POZHARSKY

CONTENTS

The Tales
of the Late
Ivan Petrovich
Belkin
edited
by A.P.

Original title
of first edition (1831)
of "The Tales of Ivan Belkin"

From the Editor

Mistress Prostakova

*Aye, Sir, he was fond of listening to
tales from a child.*

Skotinin

Mitrofan takes after me.

THE DUNCE[1]

AVING undertaken to publish the tales of I. P. Belkin, now presented to the reader, we should like to preface them with a brief account of the life of the deceased author, thereby satisfying in part the legitimate curiosity of lovers of our native literature. For this purpose we appealed to Marya Alexeyevna Trafilina, the next of kin and the heiress of Ivan Petrovich Belkin. Unfortunately, however, she was unable to furnish us with any information about him, never having had the slightest acquaintance with the deceased. She advised us to apply on this subject to a certain worthy gentleman, who was a friend of Ivan Petrovich. We followed her advice, and our letter received the satisfactory reply given below. We print it without any alterations whatever, as a precious monument to a refined understanding and a touching friendship, and at the same time a perfectly adequate biographical statement:

Respected Sir,

I had the honour to receive your kind letter of the 15th of this month on the 23rd day of the same, in which you made known to me your desire to receive detailed information concerning the birth and death, the service, the home life, occupations and character of the late Ivan Petrovich Belkin, my erstwhile sincere friend and neighbour in the country. I undertake the fulfilment of your desire with the utmost satisfaction to myself, and am sending you, my dear Sir, all that I can remember of his conversation and also some observations of my own.

Ivan Petrovich Belkin was born of honourable gentlefolk in the year 1798, in the village of Goryukhino. His late father, Second-Major Pyotr Ivanovich Belkin, married the spinster Pelageya Gavrilovna, of the Trafilin family. He was not wealthy, but thrifty, and thoroughly capable of managing his practical affairs. His son received his early education from the parish clerk. To this worthy man he seems to have owed his love of reading and his taste for writing in his native tongue. In 1815 he joined a Jager infantry regiment (I cannot recall its number), in which he remained right up to 1823. His parents dying within a short time of one another, he was compelled to send in his papers and go to live in his native village of Goryukhino, on his hereditary estate.

Entering upon the management of his estate, Ivan Petrovich, owing to his inexperience and soft-heartedness, very soon let his property fall into neglect and relaxed the strict discipline maintained by his late parent. Discharging the conscientious and efficient village-elder with whom the peasants (as is their wont) were dissatisfied, he left the management of the village to his former housekeeper, who had earned his confidence by her skill in telling stories. This gullible old woman had never been able to distinguish a twenty-five-ruble note from a fifty-ruble note; the peasants, to many of whose children she was godmother, stood in no fear of her. The peasants chose a new elder, who indulged them inordinately, con-

14

niving with them to cheat their master, so that Ivan Petrovich was obliged to give up the system of corvée, substituting for it extremely low quit-rents; even so his peasants, taking advantage of their master's weakness, wheedled out of him certain quite superfluous favours in respect to the first year, and in the next year paid over two-thirds of their rents in nuts, bilberries and the like; and even here there were arrears.

As a friend of Ivan Petrovich's late father, I considered it my duty to offer my advice to the son also, and volunteered several times to restore the former order, which he had been unable to maintain by himself. For this purpose I went to visit him one day, demanded the account-books, summoned the rascal of an elder, and began looking through them in the presence of Ivan Petrovich. The youthful proprietor at first followed my investigations with the utmost attention and diligence, but when the accounts showed that during the past two years the number of peasants had increased, while that of the poultry and cattle had noticeably decreased, Ivan Petrovich was content with these preliminary calculations, and would listen to no more, and at the very moment when I had reduced the rascally elder, by my investigations and stern questions, to extreme confusion, and silenced him completely, what was my vexation to hear Ivan Petrovich snoring loudly in his chair! From that moment I ceased to interfere in the arrangements of his estate, leaving his affairs (as he did himself) to the will of the Almighty.

The friendliness of our relations was by no means affected by all this, for, while deploring his weakness and the disastrous slackness common to our young gentlefolk, I was sincerely attached to Ivan Petrovich. It would indeed have been impossible not to love so kindly and honourable a youth. And Ivan Petrovich, for his part, paid me the respect due

15

to my years, and was very fond of me. We met almost daily, up to the very end, for he valued my simple conversation, though, as regards habits, manner of thinking, and dispositions, we had very little in common.

Ivan Petrovich was extremely moderate in his tastes, avoiding all forms of indulgence; I never saw him the worse for drink (a perfect miracle this, in our parts); he had a great weakness for the female sex, but was himself as bashful as a maid.*

In addition to the tales to which you refer in your letter, Ivan Petrovich left behind a number of manuscripts, some of which are in my possession, and some of which have been used by the housekeeper for various domestic purposes. Thus, last winter, all the windows in her wing of the house were pasted up with the first part of a novel which he neveh finished. If I am not mistaken the above-mentioned tales were his first literary attempts. Most of them, according to Ivan Petrovich, are true, and were related to him by various persons.** Almost all the names are, however, fictitious, while the hamlets and villages are taken from our parts, my own village being referred to among others. This was not owing to

---

* Here follows an anecdote which we omit as superfluous. At the same time we can assure the reader it contained nothing injurious to the memory of Ivan Petrovich.

** As a matter of fact, every tale in the manuscript of I. P. Belkin bears the inscription, in the author's hand: "Told me by So-and-so (rank or title, and initials). We may cite the following for the curious: "The Postmaster" was related to him by Titular Counsellor A.G.N., "The Shot" by Colonel I.L.P., "The Undertaker" by B.V., a shop-assistant, "Blizzard" and "Lady Into Lassie" by a young lady K.I.T.

any evil intentions whatsoever, but simply to lack of imagination.

In the autumn of 1828 Ivan Petrovich caught a severe cold which developed into a high fever, and died, despite the indefatigable efforts of the local apothecary, a man of great skill, especially in the treatment of long-standing diseases, such as corns and the like. Ivan Petrovich died in my arms in his thirtieth year, and was buried in the churchyard at Goryukhino, beside his parents.

Ivan Petrovich was of middle height, had grey eyes, fair hair and a straight nose; he was light-complexioned and lean of countenance.

This is all, dear Sir, that I have been able to recollect of the life, occupations, disposition, and appearance of my late neighbour and friend. If, however, you should see fit to make any use of my letter, I would ask you to be so kind as not to mention my name; for though I greatly esteem and love men of letters I have no desire to appear in that guise myself; indeed, considering my years, it would be unbecoming.

With sincere respect, I remain. . . . .

November 16th, 1830,
Village of Nenaradovo.

Considering it a duty to respect the will of our author's friend, we proffer him our profound gratitude for the information furnished by him, and trust that our readers will appreciate the sincerity and frankness of his contribution.

A. P.

THE SHOT

We fought a duel.

BARATYNSKY[2]

*I vowed I would shoot him by right of
duel (I still owed him a shot).*

EVENING AT THE BIVOUAC[3]

I

W E WERE stationed at the small town of X. Everyone
knows what the life of an army officer is like. In
the morning, drill and the riding-school; dinner at the Regimental Commander's, or in some Jewish tavern; punch and
cards in the evening. There was not a single house open to
us in X., not a single marriageable girl. We forgathered in
one another's quarters, where there was nothing for us to look
at but one another's uniforms.

There was only one person in our circle who was not a
military man. He was about thirty-five, and we considered him
quite old. His experience gave him great advantages over us;

and in addition to this, his habitual gloom, harsh disposition and malicious tongue exercised a powerful influence on our youthful minds. His fate was shrouded in mystery; he seemed to be a Russian, and yet he bore a foreign name. At one time he had served hussars, and with every prospect of a successful career. Nobody knew what it was that had made him resign his commission and settle in a wretched little town, where he lived at the same time meanly and lavishly, going about on foot, in a worn black frock-coat, but keeping open house for all the officers of our regiment. True, his dinner consisted of two or three dishes, cooked by an ex-soldier, but champagne flowed unchecked at his table. Nobody knew what his fortune or his income was, and nobody dared to question him about them. He had a good supply of books, mostly military texts and novels, which he was always ready to lend, and never asked for again. And he himself never returned to its owner a book he had borrowed. His principal occupation was shooting from a pistol. The walls of his room were riddled with bullet-holes, and looked like the sections of a honeycomb. His rich collection of pistols was the only luxury of the wretched clay hut in which he lived. The skill which he had achieved was of the highest order, and if he had suggested shooting a pear from somebody's cap, there was not a man in our regiment who would have hesitated to place his head at his disposal. Our conversation frequently turned on the subject of duelling, but Silvio (as I will call him) never took any part in it. When asked if he had ever fought a duel he would reply curtly that he had, without entering into any details, and it was obvious that such questions displeased him. We decided that he had some unfortunate victim of his terrible skill on his conscience. It certainly never entered our heads to suspect that there was anything like cowardice in him. There are some people whose very appearance forbids such suspicions. And then an event occurred which took us all by surprise.

One day some ten of our officers were dining at Silvio's quarters. We drank about as much as usual, which is to say a great deal. After dinner we begged our host to keep the bank for us. He held out for a long time, for he seldom played cards. But at last he ordered cards to be brought in, scattered fifty or so ten-ruble pieces on the table, and began dealing out the cards. We all surrounded him, and the game was on. It was Silvio's habit to maintain absolute silence while playing, neither arguing, nor offering explanations. If the punter happened to make a mistake Silvio either paid up immediately or jotted down the surplus. We were well aware of this and allowed him to dictate his own rules. But among us was an officer lately transferred to our regiment. While playing, this man absent-mindedly raised the stakes a point; Silvio picked up a piece of chalk and, according to his wont, righted the score. The officer, thinking Silvio had made a mistake, entered into explanations. Silvio went on with the game in silence. The officer, losing patience, picked up the brush and rubbed out what he considered had been wrongly entered. Silvio picked up the chalk and wrote the figures down again. The officer, heated by the wine, the gambling, and the laughter of his comrades, considered himself mortally insulted, and seizing a brass candlestick from the table flung it at Silvio, who only just managed to evade the impact. We were greatly perturbed. Pale with rage, his eyes gleaming, Silvio rose. "Sir," he said, "be so kind as to go, and thank God that this happened in my house."

We had no doubt of the outcome, and looked upon our new comrade as a dead man. The latter went away, saying that he was ready to answer for the insult whenever it suited the gentleman in charge of the bank. The game went on a few minutes longer, but we all felt that our host could not give his mind to the cards, and one by one we took our departure, making for our respective quarters and discussing the vacancy soon to be expected.

At riding-school the next day we were asking one another if the poor lieutenant was still alive, when he suddenly made his appearance among us; we put the same question to him. He replied that he had had no word from Silvio yet. This astonished us. We went to Silvio's house, and found him firing one shot after another right in the middle of an ace-card stuck in the gate. He received us in his usual manner, without a word about the previous day's incident. Three days passed, and the lieutenant was still alive. Could it be that Silvio did not intend to fight, we asked one another in astonishment. Silvio did not fight. He contented himself with a very slight apology, and made it up with the lieutenant.

This might have lowered him considerably in the eyes of the young men. Lack of courage is the last thing to be forgiven by young people, who usually regard bravery as the supreme virtue, covering a multitude of sins. Gradually, however, the whole thing was forgotten, and Silvio regained his former influence.

I alone was unable to feel the same about him. Endowed by nature with a romantic imagination, I had formerly been more devoted than all the rest to the man whose life was such an enigma, and whom I regarded as the hero of some mysterious tale. And he was attached to me; at any rate I was the only one with whom he desisted from his usual malicious persiflage, and discussed various topics with simplicity and extraordinary charm. But the remembrance of that unfortunate

evening, when the stain on his honour was not washed out by his own volition, never left me, and prevented me from treating him as usual. I was ashamed to meet his eyes. Silvio was too clever and too experienced not to observe this and guess at its cause. It seemed to distress him, at any rate I once or twice observed in him the desire to open his heart to me. But I avoided such opportunities and Silvio left me to myself. From this time I only met him in the company of my comrades, and our former frank talks came to an end.

The pampered inhabitants of great cities can have no conception of many sensations which are familiar to the inhabitants of villages or country towns, such as, for example, the waiting for mail-day to come round again. On Tuesdays and Fridays regimental head-quarters were always crowded with officers, some expecting money, some letters, some newspapers. Letters were as a rule unsealed then and there, and items of news exchanged, so that the office presented a scene of great animation. Silvio, who received his letters through the regiment, was usually there, too. One day he was handed a letter, the seal of which he broke with an air of the utmost impatience. His eyes gleamed as he glanced swiftly over its contents. The officers, each occupied with his own letters, noticed nothing. "Gentlemen," cried Silvio, "circumstances require my instant departure. I must leave to-night. I trust you will not refuse to dine with me for the last time. I shall expect you," he continued, addressing me. "You must come!" With these words he hastened out of head-quarters, and the rest of us, agreeing to meet at Silvio's house, went each his own way.

I arrived at Silvio's house at the appointed hour and found almost the entire regiment gathered there. His things were already packed; nothing remained but the bare, bullet-riddled walls. We sat down to table; our host was in the best of spirits, and his gaiety was soon communicated to his guests. Corks popped incessantly, the wine frothed and hissed in the glasses, as we indefatigably wished the departing one a good journey and the best of luck. It was late in the evening when we rose from the table. While we were getting our caps, Silvio took leave of each one separately; taking my hand in his, he stopped me just as I was leaving. "I want to speak to you," he said in low tones. I stayed behind.

The guests had gone, and we remained alone, facing each other and lighting our pipes in silence. Silvio was preoccupied, not a trace of his spasmodic gaiety was left. His sombre pallor and gleaming eyes, and the thick smoke issuing from his mouth, made him look like a veritable demon. A few minutes passed, and then Silvio broke the silence.

"Perhaps we shall never meet again," he said. "Before parting I should like to have a talk with you. You may have remarked that I do not care much what others think of me, but I like you, and it would pain me to leave you under a false impression."

He paused and began to refill the bowl of his pipe. I looked down without uttering a word.

"You thought it strange," he continued, "that I did not demand satisfaction from that drunken fop R. You will agree that I, being entitled to choose the weapons, held his life in my hands, while my own was scarcely threatened. I might allow you to ascribe my moderation to sheer magnanimity, but I have no desire to deceive you. If I could have punished R. without endangering my own life in the least, I would never have forgiven him."

I gazed at him in astonishment. His admission quite took me aback. Silvio continued:

"Yes—I have no right to risk my life. Six years ago I was struck in the face, and my enemy is still alive."

My curiosity was strongly roused. "And you didn't fight him?" I asked. "I suppose you were parted by circumstances."

"I did fight him," replied Silvio, "and I have here a souvenir of our duel."

He rose and extracted from a cardboard box a braided red cap with a gilt tassel (the kind that the French call a *bonnet de police*). He put it on, and I saw that there was a bullet-hole in it an inch above the forehead.

"You are aware," continued Silvio, "that I once served in the Nth Hussar regiment. And you know my disposition. I am accustomed to be first in everything; but in my youth it was a passion with me. Rowdiness was the fashion in our day, and I was the greatest fire-eater in the army. We were proud of getting drunk, and I once drank the famous Burtsov, immortalized by the poet Denis Davydov,[4] under the table. Duels took place almost every minute in our regiment, and there was hardly one in which I was not either a second or an active participator. My comrades idolized me, while the regimental commanders, who were constantly changing, regarded me as an inevitable evil.

"I was calmly (or perhaps not so calmly!) enjoying my fame, when a wealthy youth, the scion of a distinguished line whom I will not name, joined the regiment. Never had I seen one so brilliant and so favoured by fortune! Figure to yourself youth, brains, looks, boisterous spirits, reckless courage, a resounding name, money which he expended lavishly, and which never seemed to come to an end, and try and imagine the impression he was bound to make on us. My title of champion was shaken. Attracted by my reputation, he tried at first to cultivate my friendship, but I received his advances coldly, and he desisted without the slightest regret. I conceived a bitter hatred for him. His popularity in the regiment and among women drove me to utter desperation. I tried to pick a quarrel with him—he capped my epigrams with epigrams of his own, which always seemed to me wittier and fresher than mine, and which were certainly infinitely more amusing. He merely jested, my shafts were poisoned. At last one evening at a ball given by a Polish landowner, seeing him the cynosure of all the ladies, especially of the lady of the house, with whom I was having an affair, I uttered some words of vulgar raillery in his ear. He flushed up and struck me in the face. Our hands flew to our sword-hilts. Ladies swooned, we were forcibly parted, and we set off to fight a duel that very night.

"It was the hour of dawn. I stood at the appointed place with my three seconds. I awaited my opponent with indescribable impatience. It was spring and the sun rose early, so it was already hot. I caught sight of him from afar. He was on foot, carrying his tunic on his sword, and accompanied by a single second. We went to meet him. He approached with his cap, full of cherries, in his hand. The seconds paced out twelve steps between us. I was to shoot first, but I was so shaken with rage that I could not rely on the steadiness of my hand, and yielded the first shot to him. But this my opponent would not agree to. It was decided to draw lots—the lot fell to him, the perpetual favourite of fortune. He took aim and shot through my cap. Then it was my turn.

At last his life was in my hands. I gazed keenly at him, trying to discern the slightest trace of anxiety. He faced my
pistol, selecting ripe cherries out of his cap and spitting out
the stones, which almost reached to where I was standing. His
coolness infuriated me. What's the good of depriving him of
his life, I thought, when he doesn't even value it? A fiendish
thought passed through my mind. I lowered the hand holding
the pistol.

" 'I see you are too busy to think of death,' I said, 'it is
your pleasure to breakfast. I do not wish to disturb you.' 'You
don't disturb me in the least,' he retorted, 'be so good as to
fire. Just as you please, however. You owe me a shot, and
I shall always be at your service.' I turned to the seconds
and told them I did not intend to shoot at the moment, and
the duel ended at that.

"I resigned from the army and retired to this little place.
Ever since, not a single day has passed without my meditating
revenge. My hour has now struck. . . ."

Silvio drew from his pocket the letter he had received in
the morning, and gave it to me to read. Somebody (his lawyer,
apparently) wrote to him from Moscow that *a certain person*
was soon to enter into holy matrimony with a beautiful
young lady.

"You have guessed," said Silvio, "who this *certain person*
is. I am going to Moscow. We will see if he meets death on
the eve of his wedding as indifferently as he once awaited it
over a capful of cherries!"

With this, Silvio rose, dashed his cap on the floor and
began pacing up and down the room like a caged tiger. I
stood quite still, and heard him out, agitated by strange and
conflicting emotions.

The servant came in to say that the horses were in readiness. Silvio pressed my hand warmly; we embraced. He got into the carriage, in which lay two trunks, one containing his pistols, the other his personal effects. We once more bade each other farewell, and the horses galloped off.

II

Several years passed, and domestic circumstances compelled me to take up my abode in a poverty-stricken village in the X. district. While occupied with the management of my estate, I never ceased to sigh for my former noisy, care-free life. The thing I found it hardest of all to accustom myself to, was the utter solitude of the evenings in autumn and winter. Till the dinner-hour I contrived, somehow or other, to fill up my time, talking to the village-elder, driving about the estate to see how the work was doing, or visiting newly-started enterprises. But as soon as dusk began to fall I did not know what to do with myself. I already knew by heart the contents of the few books which I had discovered in various closets, and in the store-room. The housekeeper Kirilovna had related her store of tales again and again; the songs of the women reduced me to a state of melancholy. I might have taken to drinking bitters, if they had not made my head ache. Moreover I have to freely admit that I was afraid of becoming a drunkard out of sheer ennui, that is to say, the worst of all drunkards, of whom I have seen innumerable examples in our district. My only neighbours were two or three of these unfortunates, whose conversation consisted mainly in hiccoughs and sighs. Solitude was more tolerable than such company.[5]

Four versts away was the rich estate of the Countess B. But no one lived there except the steward, the countess having visited her estate only once, during the first year of her marriage, and then stayed not much over a month. But during the second spring of my seclusion it was rumoured that the countess and her husband intended to visit their estate in the summer. And in the beginning of June they actually arrived.

The arrival of a wealthy neighbour marks an era in the lives of country-dwellers. The landowners and their domestics talk about it for two months before the occurrence and three years after. In my own case I admit that the tidings of the arrival of a young and beautiful neighbour had a powerful effect on me. I burned with impatience to see her, and set off for the village of C. after dinner on the first Sunday after her arrival, to introduce myself to their Excellencies as their nearest neighbour and most humble servant.

The footman led me to the count's study and went away to announce me. The spacious study was furnished with the utmost luxury; against the walls were well-filled book-shelves, each with a bronze bust on the top. Above the marble fireplace was a great mirror; the floor was carpeted with green cloth, over which rugs were scattered. Having grown unaccustomed to luxury in my humble nook, and long ceased to witness the wealth of others, I was seized with timidity, and awaited the count with nervous anxiety, as a suitor from the provinces awaits the coming of the Minister. The door opened, admitting an exceedingly handsome man of about thirty-two. The count approached me with a cordial and friendly air. Endeavouring to recover my composure, I was about to introduce myself, but he forestalled me. We sat down. His conversation, which was courteous and easy, soon vanquished the shyness born of my long solitude; I was just beginning to feel at my ease, when the countess entered, and I was seized with

31

still greater embarrassment than before. She was indeed a lovely creature. The count introduced me. I wished to appear at my ease, but the more I tried to assume a nonchalant air, the more embarrassed I felt. In order to give me time to recover my presence of mind and get used to being among strangers, they began talking to each other, treating me without ceremony, as a good neighbour. In the meanwhile I walked up and down, looking at the books and pictures. I knew very little about pictures, but there was one which attracted my attention. It depicted a Swiss landscape, but it was not the picture itself that attracted me so much as the fact that it bore the marks of two bullet-holes, one exactly over the other. "That was a good shot," I said, turning to the count. "Yes," he replied, "a remarkable shot. Are *you* a good shot?" he went on. "First-rate," I answered, glad that the talk had at last turned on a subject so close to my heart. "I wouldn't miss a card at thirty paces—from pistols I was used to, of course." "Really?" said the countess, with an air of great attention. "Could *you* hit a card at thirty paces, my love?" "We'll have a try one day," said the count. "I wasn't a bad shot in my time. But I haven't had a pistol in my hand these four years." "Oh," I remarked, "in that case I will wager Your Excellency would not be able to hit a card at twenty paces—pistol-shooting requires daily practice. I know that from experience. I used to be considered one of the best shots in our regiment. But once I passed a whole month without touching a pistol— mine were undergoing repair. And what do you think, Your Excellency? The first time I tried to shoot after that, I missed a bottle at twenty-five paces, four times running. Our captain, who was a wag and a joker, was there and he said to me: 'Anyone can see you can't bear to hit a bottle, friend.' Oh no,

32

Your Excellency must not neglect that exercise, or you'll get out of practice in no time. The best shot I ever knew used to try his hand every day, shooting at least three times before dinner. It was just as much a habit with him as a glass of vodka before a meal." The count and countess were glad that I had found my tongue. "Tell me something more about his shooting," the count asked. "I'll tell you what, Your Excellency—sometimes he would see a fly settle on the wall— I see you are laughing, Countess, but what I say is true, I swear. Well, so he would see a fly and shout out: 'Kuzka, my pistol!' and Kuzka would bring him his loaded pistol. And bang, the fly would be squashed against the wall." "Marvellous!" exclaimed the count. "What was his name?" "Silvio, Your Excellency." "Silvio!" cried the count, jumping up. "Did you know Silvio?" "Indeed I did, Your Excellency. He and I were great friends. He was received in our regiment like one of ourselves. But I haven't heard a word of him for five years now. And so Your Excellency knew him, too?" "I did. I knew him very well. Did he never tell you ... but that is hardly likely ... did he never tell you of a certain remarkable episode in his life?" "Does Your Excellency mean the time a young fop struck him in the face?" "And did he never tell you the name of that young fop?" "No, Your Excellency, he didn't," I said. Then, the truth suddenly dawning on me—"Oh, Your Excellency," I exclaimed, "forgive me! I had no idea ... was it you?" "It was," replied the count, looking extremely distressed. "And the picture with the bullet-holes is a souvenir of our last meeting. . . ." "Oh, my dear," said the countess. "Do not talk about it, I implore you. You know it always frightens me. . . ." "Ah, but I will, I will relate it all," said the count. "He knows how I insulted his friend. Let him hear how Silvio avenged himself on me." The count pulled up an arm-chair for me, and I listened with the most lively curiosity to the following narrative:

"Five years ago I got married. The first month, the honeymoon, I spent here, in this village. I owe the happiest moments of my life to this house and one of my saddest memories.

"One evening we were out riding together. My wife's horse became restive. She was alarmed, and handing the reins to me went back to the house on foot. I rode ahead. I saw a travelling carriage in the yard, and was told that there was a man waiting for me in my study who had refused to give his name, simply saying that he had business with me. I went into this room and saw in the dusk a man, covered with dust and unshaven, standing before the fire-place, just here. I went up to him, trying to remember who he was. 'Don't you know me, Count?' he said in a trembling voice. 'Silvio!' I cried, and I have to admit that I could feel my hair standing on end. 'Quite so,' he said. 'It is my turn to fire! I have come to discharge my pistol. Are you ready?' A pistol was sticking out of his breast-pocket. I measured out twelve paces, and stood over there in the corner, begging him to be quick, and fire before my wife got back. He delayed, asking for lights. Candles were brought. I locked the door and gave orders for no one to be admitted, and once more asked him to fire. He drew out the pistol and took aim. I counted the seconds.... I thought of her.... A minute of terrible suspense passed. Silvio let his hand fall. 'I regret,' said he, 'that my pistol is not loaded with cherry-stones, bullets are so heavy. I can't help feeling as if this were not a duel but murder. I'm not used to aiming at an unarmed man. Let us begin all over again— draw lots for the first shot.' My head reeled ... as far as I remember, I did not agree.... At last we loaded another

34

pistol, twisted up two lots, which he put into the cap I had once shot through. Again I drew the lucky number. 'You have the devil's own luck, Count,' he said, with a smile I shall never forget. I cannot understand what came over me, and how I could have allowed him to make me do it. . . . But I fired, and hit that picture." (The count pointed to the picture with the bullet-holes. His cheeks flamed; the countess was whiter than her shawl; I was unable to suppress an exclamation.)

"I fired," continued the count, "and thank God I missed. Then Silvio . . . he was a terrible sight at that moment . . . began to take aim at me. Suddenly the door opened, and Masha rushed in, shrieking and throwing herself on my shoulder. The sight of her gave me back my presence of mind. 'My dear,' I said to her, 'don't you see we are joking? What a state you are in! Go and have a drink of water, and then come back to us. I want to introduce my old friend and comrade to you.' Masha still did not believe me. 'Tell me, is it true what my husband says?' she asked, turning to the formidable Silvio. 'Is it true that you are both only joking?' 'He is always joking, Countess,' replied Silvio. 'Once he struck me in the face just for a joke, he shot through my cap for a joke, and just now he missed his aim for a joke. And now I feel inclined to have a joke. . . .' With these words he again made as if to aim at me—in front of her! Masha threw herself at his feet. 'Get up, Masha, for shame!' I cried in a frenzy. 'And you, Sir, will you stop mocking at an unfortunate woman? Do you intend to fire, or do you not?' 'I do not,' replied Silvio. 'I have received satisfaction. I have seen you anxious, alarmed. I made you shoot at me, and I have had enough. You will remember me. I leave you to your conscience.' Here he made as if to go, but standing in the doorway he glanced at the picture I had hit, fired at it almost without taking aim, and vanished. My wife was in a swoon. My servants, who did not dare to detain him, merely looked aghast at him. He stepped into the porch, called to his coachman, and was gone before I had time to realize what had happened."

The count said no more. And thus it was that I discovered the end of the tale, the beginning of which once made such an impression on me. I never again met its hero. It is said that Silvio led a detachment during the Alexander Ipsilanti[6] rising, and was killed in the battle of Skulyani.

Blizzard

The steads fly o'er the rugged ground,
Trampling the snow beneath their hoofs. . . .
When lo! amidst the solitude
Appeared the lonely house of God.

. . . . .

And sudden blizzard covers all
Tho snow descends in whirling flakes;
And a fable crow with whistling wing
Sweeps low above the bounding sleigh.
Its cry prophetic bodes no good!
The flying horses strain their sight,
Peering into the distant gloom,
Their manes erect in fear.

ZHUKOVSKY

OWARDS the end of the year 1811, that never-to-be-for-gotten period of our history, there lived in his estate of Nenaradovo the worthy Gavrila Gavrilovich R. He was known throughout the district for his hospitality and kindliness; neighbours visited him incessantly, to eat, drink and play Boston for five-kopek stakes with his wife, while some came to look at their daughter Marya Gavrilovna, a maiden who was pale, slender and seventeen. She was considered a good match, and there were many who hoped to win her for themselves or their sons.

Marya Gavrilovna had been brought up on French novels, and consequently was in love. The object of her choice was an ensign with a pale countenance, on leave of absence in his hereditary village. It goes without saying that the young man burned with equal passion, and that the parents of his beloved, observing their mutual inclination, forbade their daughter to think of him, and received him as coldly as if he were a retired assize-magistrate.

Our lovers kept up a correspondence, and met every day in the solitude of a pine copse, or at an ancient chapel. There they vowed eternal love, bewailed their sad lot, and made all sorts of plans. As a result of such correspondence and conversation they came (naturally enough) to the following conclusion: since we cannot exist without each other, and cruel parents stand in the way of our happiness, why not dispense with their consent? It will easily be imagined that the young man was the first to arrive at this happy thought, and that it greatly pleased the romantic fancy of Marya Gavrilovna.

Winter came, putting an end to their meetings: but this only made their correspondence more animated. Vladimir Nikolayevich implored his beloved in every letter to become his, to marry him in secret, live in concealment for a short time, after which they would throw themselves at the feet of her parents, whose hearts could not fail to be touched by the heroic fidelity and suffering of the lovers, and who would surely exclaim: Come to our arms, children!

Marya Gavrilovna was long in making up her mind: innumerable plans for flight were rejected. At last she agreed:

on the day appointed she was to absent herself from the supper-
table, and take refuge in her bedroom, pleading a headache.
Her maid was let into the secret. Both girls were to go into the
garden through the back-entrance, to find a waiting sleigh, get
into it and drive the five versts from Nenaradovo to the village
of Zhadrino, straight to the church, where Vladimir would
be waiting for them.

On the eve of the decisive day Marya Gavrilovna did not
sleep all night; she went through her wardrobe, making a
bundle of her linen and dresses, indited a lengthy epistle to
a certain sentimental young lady-friend of hers, and another
to her parents. She bade them farewell in the most moving
terms, ascribing her action to the overwhelming power of passion, and ending her letter with the declaration that she would
consider the moment when she would be permitted to throw
herself at the feet of her beloved parents as the happiest of
her life. Sealing both letters with a Tula seal—two flaming
hearts above an appropriate inscription—she flung herself on
her bed just before daybreak and fell into a light doze, but
was aroused every few minutes by terrible dreams. Once she
dreamed that at the very moment when she was getting into
the sleigh to drive to the church, her father stopped her,
dragging her over the snow with agonizing speed and flinging
her into a dark, bottomless dungeon . . . she plunging rapidly
downwards, her heart almost stopping; another time she
dreamed she saw Vladimir lying pale and bleeding on the
grass. Dying, he begged her in piercing accents to hasten their
marriage. . . . Visions, hideous and chaotic, passed before her
mind one after another. At last she rose, even paler than
usual, with a genuine headache. Her father and mother noted
her perturbation; their tender solicitude and incessant questions: "What is the matter with you, Masha? Are you ill,

Masha?" smote her heart. She endeavoured to allay their fears and appear cheerful, but did not succeed in this. Evening came. The thought that this was the last day she would spend in the bosom of her family, made her heart ache. She could hardly breathe; in secret she bade farewell to all the persons and objects so familiar to her. Supper was served; her heart beat violently. In a trembling voice she announced that she did not want any supper, and said good night to her father and mother. They kissed her and gave her their blessing, in the usual way; she almost wept. Once in her bedroom, she flung herself into an arm-chair and burst into tears. Her maid begged her to calm down and recover her cheerfulness. All was in readiness. Half an hour later Masha was to bid farewell forever to her parents' home, her own room, her tranquil girlhood. . . . Outside a blizzard was raging; the wind was howling, the shutters shaking and rattling; everything seemed to her like a threat or a mournful omen. Soon the whole house was wrapt in sleep. Masha covered her shoulders with a shawl, put on a warm cloak, picked up her trinket-box, and left the house by the back-door, her maid following her with two bundles. They went into the garden. The blizzard had not abated; the wind blew in their faces, as if endeavouring to stop the youthful sinner. It was all they could do to get to the end of the garden. In the road a sleigh was awaiting them. The horses, chilled through, could hardly stand still; Vladimir's coachman was pacing up and down in front of the shafts, in his efforts to control the mettlesome steeds. He helped the young lady and her maid to seat themselves and settle their bundles and trinket-box in the sleigh, gathered the reins into his hands, and the horses sprang forward with a will. Leaving our heroine to the mercy of fate and the skill of the coachman Tereshka, we will turn to our youthful lover.

Vladimir had been driving from place to place all day. In the morning he visited the priest at Zhadrino and persuaded him, not without difficulty, to comply with his request; then he went in search of witnesses from among the neighbouring landowners. The first one he visited, Dravin, a forty-year-old retired cornet, gave his consent readily, declaring that the adventure reminded him of former times and Hussar pranks. He persuaded Vladimir to stay and dine with him, assuring him that there would be no difficulty in finding the other two witnesses. Indeed, immediately after dinner, land-surveyor Schmidt, moustached and spurred, made his appearance, accompanied by the son of the district police officer, a lad of some sixteen summers, who had recently entered a regiment of the Uhlans. They not only agreed to Vladimir's proposal, but they declared their readiness to sacrifice their lives for him. Vladimir embraced them warmly, and went home to make his preparations.

Dusk had long fallen. He dispatched his *troika* with his trusty Tereshka, fully instructed, to Nenaradovo, and ordering his small one-horse sleigh to be harnessed, he drove himself to Zhadrino, where, in two hours' time, Marya Gavrilovna was to arrive. The road was familiar to him, and the drive should not have taken more than twenty minutes.

But hardly had Vladimir left the village behind and found himself in open country, when the wind rose and the blizzard became so dense that he could see nothing. The road was snowed up in a minute; the surroundings vanished in a snowy haze, dim and yellowish, in the midst of which whirled white snow-flakes; the sky merged with the ground; Vladimir found himself in the middle of a field, and tried in vain to get back to the road; the horse stepped out into the unknown, now blundering into a snow-drift, now tumbling into a hollow; the sleigh was continually overturning. All Vladimir's efforts were concentrated on trying not to lose his way. But after what seemed to him half an hour, he had not reached the copse at Zhadrino. Another ten minutes or so passed, and the copse was still not to be seen. Vladimir drove over open country, criss-crossed by deep gullies. The blizzard had not subsided, and the sky was still overclouded. The horse began to show signs of fatigue, and Vladimir perspired freely, despite the fact that he was continually plunging up to his waist in snow.

At last he discovered that he had been travelling in the wrong direction. He reined in the horse and gave himself up to thought, trying to recall, to calculate, and coming to the conclusion that he ought to have turned to the right. He now did so. His horse could hardly move. He had already been over an hour on the way. Zhadrino should be not far off now. But he drove on and on and there was no end to the field—nothing but snow-drifts and gullies; the sleigh continually overturning, and continually having to be set to rights by Vladimir. Time passed. Vladimir began to feel intense anxiety.

At last something black loomed to one side. Vladimir turned the horse towards it. Approaching it, he saw a copse before him. Thank God, he thought, now I am nearly there. He drove past the copse, hoping to find himself immediately on the familiar road, or to skirt the copse—Zhadrino lay just beyond it. He soon found the road and drove on beneath the gloom of the trees, their branches stripped bare by winter. The wind could not rage here; the road was smooth; the horse took fresh heart, and Vladimir recovered his composure.

But he drove on and on and Zhadrino did not come into sight; there was no end to the copse. Vladimir realized with horror that he was in an unfamiliar wood. Overcome by despair, he struck the horse; the poor beast broke into a trot, but quickly tired and in fifteen minutes proceeded at a footpace, despite all the efforts of the unhappy Vladimir.

The wood gradually became less dense, and at last Vladimir emerged from it; Zhadrino was not in sight. It seemed to him that it must now be about midnight. Tears streamed down his cheeks; he drove at random. The storm had abated, the clouds dispersed, and before him lay a plain, covered by a white, billowy carpet of snow. It was a fairly clear night. Not far off he could see a hamlet, a mere cluster of homesteads. Vladimir drove up to it. He jumped out of the sleigh in front of the first hut, and running up to the window, knocked. In a few minutes the wooden shutter was raised, and an old man thrust out his grey beard. "What do you want?" "Is it far from here to Zhadrino?" "Is it far to Zhadrino?" "Yes, yes, is it far?" "Not far; about ten versts." At this reply Vladimir tore his hair and stood stock still, like a man who had just heard his death sentence.

"And where may you come from?" asked the old man. Vladimir had not the strength to answer his questions. "Can you find me a horse to get to Zhadrino, old man?" he asked. "As if we had any horses!" replied the peasant. "Well, couldn't you find me someone to show me the way, then? I'll pay whatever he asks." "Wait a minute," said the old man, lowering the shutter. "I'll send my son; he'll show you the way." Vladimir waited. Hardly a minute had passed before he again knocked at the window. The shutter was raised, the beard reappeared. "What d'you want?" "Where's your son?" "He's coming, he's putting on his boots. Come in and warm yourself if you're cold." "No, thanks—make your son hurry up."

The door creaked; a youth holding a staff came out, and walked ahead, sometimes pointing out the road, sometimes stopping to look for it, snowed up as it was with heavy drifts. "What's the time?" Vladimir asked him. "Why, it'll soon be light," the young fellow replied. Vladimir uttered not another word.

The cocks were crowing and it was already light when they got to Zhadrino. The church was locked. Vladimir paid off his guide and went to the home of the priest. There was no *troika* standing in the yard. And what tidings awaited him!

But we will now return to the worthy proprietors of Nenaradovo and see what is going on there.

Nothing at all!

The old folk woke up and went into their drawing-room, Gavrila Gavrilovich in his night-cap and flannel jacket, Praskovya Petrovna in a wadded robe. The samovar was brought in and Gavrila Gavrilovich sent a girl to ask how Marya Gavrilovna was, and how she had slept. The girl returned, saying that the young lady had slept badly but that she now felt better and would soon be in the drawing-room. And at that moment the door opened and Marya Gavrilovna came in, and greeted her Papa and Mama.

"How is your head, Masha?" asked Gavrila Gavrilovich. "Better, Papa," replied Masha. "It must have been the stove that made it ache, Masha," said Praskovya Petrovna. "Perhaps it was, Mama," replied Masha.

The day passed uneventfully, but that night Masha fell ill. A doctor was sent for from the neighbouring town. He arrived the next evening and found the patient delirious. A violent fever set in, and the unhappy girl lay two weeks between life and death.

No one in the house knew that flight had been intended. The letters written the evening before had been burned; Masha's maid said not a word to anyone, fearing the wrath of her master. The priest, the retired cornet, the bewhiskered land-surveyor and the youthful uhlan were discreet for reasons of their own. Tereshka the coachman never let fall an unnecessary word, even when tipsy. And so the secret shared by more than half a dozen conspirators was kept. But Marya Gavrilovna herself gave away her secret in her uninterrupted delirium. Her words were, however, so inarticulate that her mother, who never left her bedside, was only able to make out from them that her daughter was hopelessly enamoured of Vladimir Nikolayevich, and that this love was probably the cause of her illness. She consulted her husband and a few of the neighbours, and at last it was unanimously agreed that Marya Gavrilovna's fate was probably predestined, that there is no escape from fate, that poverty is no crime, that one has to live not with money-bags but with a human being, and so on. Platitudes are exceedingly helpful when we cannot find much justification for our actions.

In the meantime the girl gradually recovered. Vladimir had not been seen in the house of Gavrila Gavrilovich for a long time. He had been frightened off by the reception usually accorded him. Now he was sent for, and informed of his unexpected happiness—consent to his marriage. But what was the amazement of the owners of Nenaradovo when in reply to their invitation they received a half-crazy letter from the young man. He assured them that he would never again cross their threshold, and asked them to forget an unhappy wight, for whom the last remaining hope was death. A few days later they learned that he had gone back to the army. This was in the year 1812.

It was long before anyone ventured to tell the convalescent Masha of this. She herself never mentioned Vladimir. A few months later, discovering his name amongst those decorated for bravery, and dangerously wounded after the battle of Borodino, she swooned, and it was feared that the fever would set in again. But the swoon, thank God, had no evil consequences.

She was soon visited by a fresh sorrow—her father gave up the ghost, leaving her heiress to his whole estate. But her heritage did not console her; she sincerely shared the grief of poor Praskovya Petrovna, vowing never to part from her; they both left Nenaradovo, with its melancholy associations, and went to live on their estate in the village of X.

Here also there were plenty of suitors hovering around the charming and wealthy heiress, but she never gave any of them the slightest encouragement. Her mother sometimes tried to persuade her to choose a life-mate, but Marya Gavrilovna only shook her head and became pensive. Vladimir was no longer among the living; he had died in Moscow, on the eve of the French entry into the city. Masha held his memory sacred; at any rate she preserved everything that might remind her of him—the books he had once read, his drawings, the music and verses he had copied out for her. The neighbours, learning of this, were astounded at her constancy, and awaited with curiosity the hero who was fated to triumph finally over the mournful fidelity of this chaste Artemis.

In the meantime the war came to a victorious end and our regiments returned from foreign parts. The people ran out of their houses to meet them. The bands played songs captured from the enemy—*Vive Henri Quatre*, Tyrolese waltzes, and arias from *La Joconde*. Officers who had joined the campaign as mere lads, returned matured by the air of the battle-

field, and hung with crosses. Soldiers chatted gaily to one another, besprinkling their speech with French and German words. Unforgettable days! Days of glory and enthusiasm! How violently the Russian heart beat at the word *native land*! How sweet were the tears of reunion! How unanimously we combined feelings of national pride with love for the tsar! And what a moment it was for him!

The women, the women of Russia, were inimitable in those days. Their habitual frigidity deserted them. The enthusiasm was veritably intoxicating, when, meeting the conquerors,

> *The women cried: Hurrah!*
> *And threw their bonnets in the air!*[8]

What officer of those days but admits that he was indebted to some Russian woman for his best, most precious reward?

During this dazzling period Marya Gavrilovna lived with her mother in the gubernia of X., and did not see how the two capital cities celebrated the return of the troops. But the general enthusiasm may be said to have been still greater in the uyezds and villages. The appearance of an officer in such places was always triumphant, and the lover in a frock-coat had a hard time of it.

We have already stated that, despite her coldness, Marya Gavrilovna was surrounded by suitors as before. But all were forced to retreat when a wounded colonel of the Hussars, Burmin by name, made his appearance in her stronghold with a St. George's cross in his button-hole and a countenance of *interesting pallor*, as the local young ladies put it. He was about twenty-six years old. He was on leave of absence on his estate, which was quite close to the property of Marya Gavrilovna. Marya Gavrilovna showed him great preference.

In his presence her usual melancholy yielded to a certain liveliness. There was no hint of coquetry in her behaviour towards him; but the poet, observing her, might have said:

Se amor non è che dunque?...

Burmin was certainly a most prepossessing young man. His was precisely the kind of mind which women like—decorous, attentive, without the slightest pretensions, and tinged with easy mockery. In the presence of Marya Gavrilovna he bore himself with simplicity and freedom; but whatever she said or did, his thoughts and his glances invariably followed her. He seemed to be very quiet and discreet, but rumour had it that at one time he had been a fast liver, and this did him no harm in the eyes of Marya Gavrilovna who (like most young women) gladly forgave pranks betraying audacity and ardour.

But it was the reserve of the youthful hussar which, more than anything else—more than his gentle manners, his pleasing conversation, his interesting pallor, his bandaged arm—fired her with curiosity and stirred her fancy. She could not help realizing that she had made a great impression on him; and no doubt he, with his brains and experience, had already observed that she was far from indifferent to him—how was it then that she had not yet seen him at her feet, and heard his declaration of love? What was it that restrained him? The diffidence inseparable from genuine love? Pride? Or was it the cunning of an experienced lady's man? He was an enigma for her. After much thought she decided that diffidence was the sole cause of his reserve, and took it upon herself to encourage him by still more marked attentions and, when occasion arose, even by a display of tenderness. She thought out an issue that should be altogether unexpected, and impatiently awaited the moment of romantic declaration. A mystery of any sort is always exasperating to the heart of woman. Her military manoeuvres were crowned with success, at least to the extent that Burmin sank into such reveries, and his black eyes dwelt so ardently on Marya Gavrilovna's face, that the decisive moment seemed to be imminent. The neighbours were already talking of the wedding as of a settled affair, and the good Praskovya Petrovna rejoiced that her daughter had at last found a suitor worthy of her.

One day the old lady was sitting in her drawing-room spreading out the cards for *grande patience*, when Burmin entered and asked for Marya Gavrilovna. "She's in the garden," answered the old lady. "Go to her, and I'll stay here and wait for you both." Burmin went out and the old lady crossed herself, thinking: "Perhaps everything will be settled to-day."

Burmin found Marya Gavrilovna at the pond, beneath a willow-tree, a book in her hand and in a white dress, just like the heroine of a novel. After the usual inquiries, Marya Gavrilovna purposely refrained from keeping up the conversation, thus intensifying their mutual embarrassment, which could only be removed by a sudden and determined declaration. And this is what happened. Burmin, conscious of the awkwardness of his situation, informed her that he had long been seeking an opportunity to lay bare his heart before her, and requested a moment of her attention. Marya Gavrilovna shut her book and lowered her eyelids as a sign of consent.

"I love you," said Burmin. "I love you passionately." (Marya Gavrilovna blushed and let her head droop still lower.) "I acted indiscreetly in yielding to the delightful habit, the habit of seeing and hearing you daily...." (Marya

Gavrilovna was reminded of St. Preux's first letter.) "It is too late for me to resist my destiny; the memory of you, your sweet, incomparable image, will henceforth be the torment and joy of my whole life; but there still remains for me to fulfil a painful obligation, and disclose to you a terrible secret, which will place an insuperable barrier between us...." Marya Gavrilovna interrupted him eagerly: "It always existed ... I could never have become your wife...." "I know," he replied softly. "I know that you once loved another, but death, and three years of grief.... Dear, kind Marya Gavrilovna, do not seek to deprive me of my only consolation! The thought that you might have consented to make my happiness if ... be silent, I pray you, be silent! You torture me. I know, I feel, that you would have been mine, but—I am an unfortunate individual—I am a married man!"

Marya Gavrilovna glanced at him in astonishment.

"I am married," continued Burmin. "I have been married these four years and know not who my wife is, or where she is, or if I am destined ever to meet her."

"What!" exclaimed Marya Gavrilovna. "How very strange! Go on; I will tell you later ... but go on, I implore you!"

"Early in the year 1812," said Burmin, "I was hastening to Vilna, where our regiment was stationed. Arriving at a posting station late one evening, I ordered fresh horses to be harnessed immediately, when a terrible blizzard sprang up all of a sudden and the keeper of the station and the drivers counselled me to wait for it to pass. I heeded their advice, but a strange feeling of anxiety overcame me; it was as if I was being urged on. The blizzard did not become any less violent; I lost patience and again gave orders for horses to be harnessed, and set out in the teeth of the storm. The driver took

it into his head to go by the river, which should have shortened the journey some three versts. The banks were snowed up;
the driver went past the place where we should have gone on
to the road, and we found ourselves in an unfamiliar neighbourhood. The storm showed no sings of subsiding; I saw a
light and told the driver to go towards it. We arrived at a village; there was a light in the wooden church. The door was open
and there were several sleighs drawn up inside the fence; people were moving about inside the porch. 'This way! This way!'
shouted several voices. I told the driver to go up to the church.
'What on earth delayed you?' said someone to me. 'The bride
is in a faint; the priest doesn't know what to do; we were
just going to go home. Come in quick!' I leaped from the
sleigh without a word and entered the church, which was
faintly illuminated by a few candles. A young girl was seated
on a bench in a dark corner; another was rubbing her temples.
'God be thanked,' said this latter. 'You've only just come in
time. You have almost killed my young lady.' An old priest
approached me with the question: 'Shall we begin?' 'Begin,
Father, begin,' I answered abstractedly. The girl was helped
to her feet. She seemed to me quite pretty . . . inexplicable,
unpardonable levity. . . . I stood beside her at the altar;
the priest was in a hurry; three men and a serving-
maid supported the bride, and gave thought to no one else.
We were made man and wife. 'Kiss!' they told us. My wife
turned her pale countenance towards me. I was just going to
kiss her. She shrieked: 'Oh, it is not he! It is not he!' and
fell down unconscious. The witnesses directed a scrutinizing
gaze upon me. I turned, left the church all unhindered,
dashed into my sleigh, and shouted: 'On!' "

"Dear God!" cried Marya Gavrilovna. "And you do not
know what became of your unfortunate wife?"

"No," replied Burmin. "I do not know the name of the village where I was married; I do not remember what posting station I came from. At the time I ascribed so little importance to my reprehensible prank that I fell asleep as we left the church behind, and did not wake up till the next morning, at the third posting station. The servant who was then with me died during the campaign, so I have no hope of seeking out the person I mocked so cruelly and who is now herself so cruelly revenged."

"Good God!" said Marya Gavrilovna, seizing him by the sleeve. "So it was you! And you didn't recognize me!"

Burmin turned pale . . . and threw himself at her feet.

The

UNDERTAKER

Do not we coffins everywhere behold,
Those grey hairs of our ageing universe?

DERZHAVIN[9]

HE LAST of the domestic effects of undertaker Adrian Prokhorov had been loaded on to the hearse, and the pair of lean horses trudged for the fourth time from Basman- naya Street to Nikitskaya Street, where the undertaker had moved with his entire household. Locking up the shop, he nailed an announcement over the entrance, to the effect that the house was to be let or sold, and set off on foot for his new abode. As he approached the yellow walls of the house which had so long been the object of his desires, and which he had at last bought for a substantial sum, the old undertaker dis- covered to his surprise that he felt no joy. Stepping over the unfamiliar threshold into the new dwelling, where all was as yet chaos, he sighed for the rickety hovel in which, during the course of eighteen years, the strictest order had prevailed; chiding his two daughters and the serving-maid for their slowness, he began to help them. Order was rapidly restored; the iconostas, the china-closet, the table, the couch and the bed were all installed in their several corners in the back-room; the property of the master of the house—coffins of all colours and dimensions, and wardrobes full of mourning head-gear, cloaks and torches—was stacked in the kitchen and parlour. Over the gate was hung a sign depicting a stout Cupid, bearing a torch upside down in his hand, above the inscription: "Coffins plain and coloured sold and upholstered, also let out on hir, and old coffins repaired." His daughters retired to their own chamber, and Adrian, after inspecting his new dwelling, seated himself at the window and ordered the samovar to be heated.

The well-informed reader is aware that both Shakespeare and Sir Walter Scott represented their grave-diggers as light-hearted and waggish, in order, by force of contrast, to make a greater impression on our minds. Our respect for the truth, however, prevents us from following their example, and we are obliged to admit that our undertaker's disposition was in complete accord with his dismal trade. Adrian Prokhorov was a grave and gloomy individual. On the rare occasions when he broke silence it was to reprove his daughters when he came upon them looking idly out of the window at the passers-by, or to demand an exorbitant price for the works of his hands from those who were so unfortunate (or, as the case might be, so fortunate) as to stand in need of them. And so Adrian sat at the window over his seventh cup of tea, absorbed as usual in melancholy reflections. He remembered the torrents of rain which had greeted the funeral procession of the retired brigadier the week before, just as it was passing through the toll-gate. As a consequence many cloaks had shrunk, and many hat-brims were warped. He foresaw considerable expenditure, for the ancient stock of funeral raiment in his possession was in a pitiable state. He had hoped to compensate for his losses by the funeral of old Tryukhina, the merchant's widow, who had been lingering on the verge of the grave for a whole year. But Tryukhina was dying at Razgulyai, and Prokhorov feared that the heirs, despite the promise made to him, would not trouble to send so far for him, and would come to terms with the nearest contractor.

These meditations were suddenly interrupted by three Masonic knocks at the front door. "Who's there?" cried the undertaker. The door opened, and a man, immediately recognizable as a German craftsman, entered the room and approached the undertaker with a cheerful air. "Forgive me, dear neighbour," he said, speaking broken Russian in the manner which we are still unable to hear without laughter. "Forgive me if I interrupt you, but I wish to make your acquaintance as soon as possible. I am a shoemaker, my name is Gottlieb Schultz, and I live just across the street in the little house you can see from your window. I am celebrating my silver wedding to-morrow, and I want to invite you and your daughters to come and dine with me in a friendly way." The invitation was graciously accepted. The undertaker asked the shoemaker to sit down and drink a cup of tea with him, and soon, thanks to the frank disposition of Gottlieb Schultz, they were chatting in the most friendly manner. "How goes it in your trade?" inquired Adrian. "Heigh-ho," replied Schultz. "We have our ups and downs. I can't complain. Of course my wares are not like yours—the living can do without boots, but a dead man cannot live without a coffin." "Perfectly true," agreed Adrian. "At the same time, if a living man has no money to buy boots with, he can go barefoot, saving your presence; but a dead beggar will get his coffin for nothing." The conversation proceeded in this manner a little longer, till the shoemaker rose and took leave of the undertaker, at the same time repeating his invitation.

The next day, precisely at noon, the undertaker and his daughters stepped out of the gateway of the newly-purchased house, and set off to visit their neighbour. I will not attempt to describe the Russian *kaftan* of Adrian Prokhorov, nor the European attire of Akulina and Darya, thereby deviating in this respect from the approved custom of modern novelists. It may, however, not be superfluous to remark that both damsels wore yellow hats and red slippers, which they only put on for special occasions.

The shoemaker's small room was crowded with guests, most of whom were German craftsmen with their wives and apprentices. The only Russian official present was Police Constable Yurko, a Chukhon, who, in spite of his modest rank, enjoyed the special favour of the host. For twenty-five years he had truly and faithfully pursued his calling, like Pogorelsky's famous postman.[10] The fire of 1812, destroying the ancient capital, annihilated also his yellow sentry-box. But as soon as the enemy was driven away, a new sentry-box, painted grey and adorned with white Doric columns, appeared in its place, and Yurko resumed his pacing up and down in front of it, armed *cap-à-pie*. He was acquainted with most of the Germans inhabiting the streets around Nikitsky Gate, some of whom even found themselves obliged to spend their Sunday nights in his sentry-box. Adrian hastened to make his acquaintance, regarding him as a person of whom he would certainly stand in need sooner or later, and when the guests sat down to table, these two sat next to each other. Herr and Frau Schultz and their daughter, the seventeen-year-old Lottchen, while dining with their guests, waited at table and helped the cook to dish up. Beer flowed copiously. Yurko ate for four. Adrian was not behindhand. His daughters minded their manners. The conversation, which was carried on in German, grew ever louder. Suddenly the host called for attention, and, uncorking a bottle besmeared with tar, cried out loudly, in Russian: "To the health of my good Luise!" The light champagne frothed. The host kissed the fresh-complexioned face of his middle-aged help-mate, and the guests noisily drank the health of the good Luise. "To the health of my dear guests!" announced the host, uncorking another bottle, and the guests returned their thanks, draining their glasses again. The toasts now began to follow thick and fast—they drank to the health of each person singly, toasted the city of Moscow, and a round dozen small German towns, then came toasts to all trades as such, and to each in turn, and to the health of all the craftsmen and apprentices in them. Adrian drank conscientiously, at last becoming so elated that he actually proposed a whimsical toast. Then one of the guests, a stout baker, raised his glass with the exclamation: "To the health of those for whom we work—*unserer Kundleute!*" This toast, like all the preceding ones, was drunk with cheerful unanimity. The guests began bowing to one another—the tailor bowed to the shoemaker, the shoemaker to the tailor, the baker to them both, the entire company to the baker, and so on. In the midst of these mutual salutations, Yurko turned to the undertaker, crying: "Come on, neighbour, drink the health of your dead men!" Everyone laughed but the undertaker, who took umbrage and frowned. No one noticed this, and the guests went on drinking; by the time they rose from the table the bells were ringing for vespers.

The guests dispersed at a late hour, most of them tipsy. The stout baker, and the bookbinder, whose face seemed to be "bound in crimson morocco," led the constable to his shelter with a hand under each of his arms, observing, in this instance, the Russian proverb—a debt is crowned in the payment. The undertaker arrived home angry and befuddled. "After all," he reflected aloud, "why is my trade less honourable than the others? An undertaker is not brother to the hangman, is he? What do those foreigners find to laugh at? Is an undertaker a fool in motley for them? And I was going to invite them all to my house-warming. Oh, no, I won't do that! I will invite those for whom I work—my Christian corpses." "Oh, Sir!" exclaimed the serving-maid, who was taking off his boots. "Think what you are saying! Cross yourself! Invite the dead to a house-warming! It's horrible!" "Before God, I will do it!" continued Adrian. "And to-morrow, too! Do me the honour, my benefactors, to feast with me to-morrow night. You shall share my little all." With these words the undertaker got into bed and was soon snoring.

It was still dark outside when Adrian was roused. Tryukhina, the merchant's wife, had died during the night, and a messenger from her factotum had galloped up on horseback to bring the tidings to Adrian. The undertaker rewarded him with ten kopeks for vodka, dressed hastily, hailed a *droshky* and drove to Razgulyai. Policemen were already posted at the entrance to the house of the deceased, and merchants were strutting up and down like crows sensing carrion. The corpse was laid out on a table, her countenance waxy, but the features not yet deformed by decay. Relatives, neighbours and domestics crowded round her. All the windows were open; there were candles burning; the priests were reading the prayers for the dead.

Adrian went up to the dead woman's nephew, a youthful merchant in a fashionable frock-coat, and informed him that the coffin, candles, pall, and other funereal paraphernalia would be supplied immediately in good condition. The heir thanked him absent-mindedly, remarking that he would not haggle over the price, but would trust entirely in the undertaker's good faith. The undertaker, as was his wont, vowed that he would not charge a kopek too much, after which he exchanged a significant glance with the factotum, and drove back to make his preparations. All day he drove backwards and forwards between Razgulyai and Nikitsky Gate. By evening everything was in order, and he went home on foot, dismissing the driver. It was a moonlit night. The undertaker arrived safely at Nikitsky Gate. As he was passing the Church of the Ascension our friend Yurko challenged him, and recognizing the undertaker wished him good night. The hour was late. The undertaker was approaching his house when all of a sudden it seemed to him that somebody came up to the gate, opened it, and disappeared through it. "What can it mean?" wondered Adrian. "Who else could be needing me? Is it a thief breaking in? Can it be that young men visit my little fools by night?" He even thought of calling his friend Yurko to his aid. Just then another person approached the gate and was about to enter, but catching sight of the undertaker hurrying towards the house, he stood still and raised his cocked hat. Adrian fancied he knew the face, though in his haste he had not been able to examine it closely. "You were coming to see me,"

63

he panted. "Step in, please." "Don't stand on ceremony, Friend," said the unknown in hollow tones. "You go in first— show your guests the way." Adrian was in much too great a hurry to stand on ceremony. The gate was unlatched, and he went up the steps to the house, the other following him. It seemed to Adrian that there were people moving about in his rooms. "What the deuce does it all mean?" he thought, hastening to let himself in, and ... his knees gave way. The room was full of corpses. Through the window the moon lit up their yellow and blue visages, their fallen mouths, dim, half-shut eyes and peaked noses. ... Adrian recognized with horror people whom he had assisted to bury, and in the one who entered with him he beheld the brigadier buried during the pouring rain. They all, ladies and gentlemen alike, clustered round the undertaker, with bows and words of greeting, with the exception of one poor fellow buried free of charge not long before, who did not come near, but stood humbly in a corner of the room as if ashamed of his ragged attire. All but he were decently attired, the women in ribboned caps, the defunct officials in uniforms, but unshaven, the merchants in their best robes. "You see, Prokhorov," said the brigadier, speaking on behalf of the whole company, "we have all risen to accept your invitation. Only those who are quite helpless, who have completely decayed, have stayed behind, and those who are nothing but fleshless bones, but one of these latter could not resist coming, so anxious was he to visit you. ..." Just then a small skeleton elbowed its way through the crowd and approached Adrian. Its fleshless visage leered affectionately at Adrian. Straps of bright green and red cloth and threadbare linen clung here and there to it, as to a pole, and its shin-bones rattled in high riding-boots, like a pestle in a mortar. "Don't you recognize me, Prokhorov," said the skeleton.

"Don't you remember retired Sergeant of the Guard Pyotr Petrovich Kurilkin, the man you sold your first coffin to (a deal one, but you said it was oak), in 1799?" With these words the skeleton extended his arms in a bony embrace, but Adrian, mustering up all his strength, cried out and pushed him away. Pyotr Petrovich swayed and fell to the ground, a mere heap of disjointed bones. A hum of indignation arose from the corpses. All were anxious to defend the honour of their comrade, advancing upon Adrian with curses and threats, and the unfortunate host, deafened by their cries, and almost crushed by their onslaught, lost his presence of mind and in his turn fell unconscious upon the bones of the deceased sergeant of the guard.

The sun's rays were already lighting up the bed on which the undertaker lay. At last he opened his eyes and saw before him the servant-maid blowing on the embers in the samovar. Adrian remembered with horror the events of the night. Tryukhina, the brigadier, and Sergeant Kurilkin vaguely haunted his imagination. He waited in silence for the maid to open the conversation and tell him what the consequences of the nocturnal adventure had been.

"How late you slept, Adrian Prokhorovich, Sir," said Aksinya, handing him his morning robe. "Our neighbour the tailor came to see you, and the police constable ran in to say that it was the police inspector's name-day to-day, but you were asleep, and we didn't like to wake you."

"And did anyone come from the late widow Tryukhina?"

"Tryukhina? Why? Is she dead?"

"What a fool you are! Didn't you help me make the preparations for her funeral yesterday?"

"Have you gone mad, Sir, or are the fumes of yesterday's drinking still hanging about you? There wasn't any funeral yesterday! You feasted at the German's all day and came back drunk, and fell on to your bed and you've been asleep up till now, and the bell has stopped tolling for service."

"Have I?" exclaimed the undertaker, in relief.

"Of course you have," replied the maid.

"In that case, hurry up with the tea, and call my daughters."

The
POSTMASTER

He was a Civic Counsellor,
And the despot of a posting station.

PRINCE VYAZEMSKY[11]

how me the man who has never cursed the master of a posting station, or who has never wrangled with one; the man, who, in a moment of fury, has not demanded the fatal volume in which to enter useless complaints of arbitrary behaviour, rudeness and unpunctuality; who does not consider postmasters as monsters in human form, as bad as certain defunct officials, or at any rate no better than the Murom robbers. We will endeavour to be just, however, and to put ourselves in their place, and then, perhaps, we shall judge them with much greater indulgence. What is a postmaster? He is a veritable martyr among petty officials, protected from blows and cuffs by nothing but this official rank of his, and even this does not always save him (I appeal to the conscience of my readers). And how difficult is the position of this despot, as Prince Vyazemsky playfully calls him? Is not his work veritable hard labour? No rest either by day or by night! The traveller pours out all the vexations accumulated during the tedious journey upon the postmaster. The weather is atrocious, the roads abominable, the driver stubborn, the horses lazy— and for all this the postmaster must take the blame. The traveller who enters his poor dwelling regards him as a foe; and the postmaster is fortunate if he succeeds in soon getting rid of the uninvited guest. And if there should happen to be no horses available! Heavens, what oaths, what threats are showered on his head! He is forced to run from house to house in rain and mud; he goes out into the porch while the storm rages and the frosts of January prevail, just to get a moment's respite from the shouts and pushes of the irate traveller. A general arrives, and the trembling postmaster gives him his last two *troikas,* one of which was being reserved for the mail-coach. The general departs, without so much as a word of thanks. Five minutes later comes the sound of bells and a state-messenger flings on the table an order for fresh horses. Weigh all these circumstances, and instead of indignation, your hearts will be filled with sincere sympathy. A few more words on this subject: I have travelled all over Russia in the course of twenty years. I know almost all the posting routes; I am acquainted with several generations of drivers; there is scarcely a single postmaster whom I do not know, and with whom I have not had dealings; I hope at no distant time to publish the interesting stock of observations I have accumulated while travelling; but for the present I will merely state that the race of postmasters has been grossly misrepresented to the public. These much abused postmasters are as a rule peaceable folk, of an accommodating disposition, sociably inclined, with no exaggerated sense of what is due to them, and by no means grasping. Much that is curious and instructive may be gleaned from their conversation, which many esteemed travellers make a great mistake in neglecting. For my own part, I admit I prefer it to the speeches of your second-rate official, travelling on government business.

It will easily be guessed that I have friends among the estimable class of postmasters. Indeed there is one of them whose memory is very precious to me. Circumstances brought us together at a certain period of my life and it is his story that I now intend to relate to my indulgent readers.

In May of 1816 I chanced to travel in the province of X., by a route which no longer exists. I held the rank of a petty official, and travelled post, my means only sufficing for two horses. This caused postmasters to treat me with scant ceremony, and I frequently had to take by force that which I considered to be mine by right. Being young and impetuous I was indignant at the baseness and pusillanimity of some postmaster who gave away to some high official the horses which had been prepared for my use. It took me just as long to get used to being passed over during one of the courses at the Governor's table by some perspicacious lout of a waiter. Now both these situations seem to me quite in the order of things. After all, what would become of us if for the rule, so universally accepted, *let rank yield to rank,* another were to be substituted, for instance—*let mind yield to mind?* What disputes would arise! And whom would the domestics have to serve first? But I will return to my narrative.

It was a hot day. Three versts from the posting station of X. a light drizzle began, and a minute later I was soaked to the skin by a downpour. On arriving at the station my first care was to change my clothes as quickly as possible, my second to ask for tea. "Hey, Dunya!" cried the postmaster. "Get the samovar ready, and go and fetch some cream." In response to these words a girl of some fourteen summers emerged from behind a partition-wall and scampered to the porch. I was struck by her beauty. "Is that your daughter?" I asked the postmaster. "Yes," he replied with an air of complacency. "And she's so clever, so quick, just like her dear mother before her." He began then and there copying out my order and I fell to examining the pictures which adorned his humble but neat and clean dwelling. They illustrated the story of the Prodigal Son. In the first picture a venerable old man in night-cap and dressing-gown was bidding farewell to a restless youth who was hastily receiving his blessing and a bag of money. Another displayed in vivid detail the dissolute conduct of the young man, who was depicted seated at a table surrounded by false friends and shameless women. Then came a picture of the ruined youth in a ragged cloak and cocked hat, herding swine and sharing their meal; his face expressed profound melancholy and contrition. The last of the series showed his return to his father; the good old man, still in his night-cap and dressing-gown, ran out to meet him; the prodigal son knelt at his feet; in the background could be seen the cook slaughtering the fatted calf, and the older brother asking the servants the reason for these rejoicings. I read the appropriate German couplets beneath each picture. All this is still fresh in my memory, together with the pots of balsam and the bed with the bright-patterned curtain and other objects by which I was then surrounded. I can still see before me the master of the house himself, a man of about fifty, hale and cheerful, his long green frock-coat adorned with three medals dangling from faded ribbons.

Hardly had I paid off my old driver, when Dunya came
back with the samovar. The little coquette was not slow to
observe the impression she had made on me, and lowered
her great blue eyes demurely. I entered into conversation
with her and she answered without the slightest signs of embarrassment, like a girl who had seen something of the
world. I offered her father a glass of punch. Dunya, I handed
a cup of tea, and we all three chatted together as if we had
known one another for ages.

The horses were in readiness, but I was loath to part
from the postmaster and his daughter. At last I took leave
of them, the father wished me a good journey, and the
daughter saw me to my carriage. I stopped in the porch and
asked her to allow me to kiss her. Dunya consented.... I
can pass in review innumerable kisses,

Since I began this pastime to enjoy,
but not one of them has left such a delightful and lasting
memory.

Several years passed, and circumstances again conspired
to take me along the same route, to the same places. I remembered the postmaster's daughter, and rejoiced at the thought
that I should see her once more. And then I reflected that
the old postmaster might have been dismissed, and that
Dunya was probably married by now. The thought of the
death of the one or the other also flashed through my mind,
and I approached the posting station of X. with melancholy
forebodings.

My horses drew up before the postmaster's little house.
Going into the room I immediately recognized the pictures
illustrating the story of the Prodigal Son. The table and bed
were in their old places, but there were no longer flowers on
the window-sill, and everything in the room spoke of decay

73

and neglect. The postmaster was asleep covered by a sheep-skin coat. My arrival woke him, and he sat up.... It was Samson Vyrin himself, but how he had aged! While he was copying out my order I noticed his grey hair, the deep lines in his unshaven cheeks and his bowed shoulders, and could not contain my astonishment that three or four years should have transformed a robust man into a frail ancient. "Don't you know me?" I asked. "You and I are old friends." "Quite possible," he replied morosely. "It's a busy route, a great many travellers come here." "And how is your Dunya?" I continued. The old man frowned. "God knows," he said. "Is she married, then?" I asked. The old man pretended not to have heard my question, and went on reading over my order in a whisper. I discontinued my questions and asked to have the kettle put on. I was beginning to feel the prick-ings of curiosity, and hoped that punch would loosen my old friend's tongue.

I was not mistaken—the old man did not reject the proffered glass. I observed that rum dispersed his gloominess. By the second glass he became talkative, remembering, or at least pretending to remember, who I was, and I learned from his lips a tale which at the time interested and moved me strangely.

"So you knew my Dunya?" he began. "Ah, who did not know her! Ah, Dunya! Dunya! What a girl she was! Every-one who came here used to praise her, no one had a word to say against her. The ladies used to give her presents—some a kerchief, some a pair of ear-rings. When gentlemen came to the posting station they would stop on purpose, as if for dinner or supper, but really for the sake of looking at her a little longer. However angry a gentleman might be, he would calm down at the sight of her, and speak graciously to me. You will hardly believe it, but couriers and state-messengers would talk to her by the half-hour. My home depended on her—she found time to clean house, to cook, to do everything. And I, old fool, could not take my eyes off her, could not contain my joy in her. Did not I love my Dunya, did not I cherish my child? Did not she have an easy life? But you can't stave off disaster by prayers—there is no escape from destiny." Here he began to give me a detailed account of his misfortune.

Three years before, one wintry evening when the postmaster was ruling himself a new ledger, and his daughter was sitting behind the partition making a dress, a *troika* drew up and a traveller in a Circassian cap and military great-coat, and a thick muffler, entered the room and demanded horses. The horses were all out. On hearing this, the traveller raised his voice and his whip, but Dunya, who was familiar with such scenes, came running out from behind the partition, and addressed the traveller graciously, asking him if he would like something to eat. The appearance of Dunya produced its usual effect. The traveller's rage left him; he consented to wait for horses and ordered supper. After taking off his wet shaggy fur cap, unwinding his muffler, and throwing off his great-coat, he was seen to be a slender young hussar with a small black moustache. He made himself quite at home in the postmaster's house, and was soon chatting gaily with the postmaster and his daughter. Supper was served. Meanwhile the horses had returned and the postmaster ordered them to be harnessed to the traveller's sleigh, without even being fed. But when he got back to his room he found the young man lying almost unconscious on the bench. He felt faint, his head ached, he was not fit to travel.... There was no help for it! The postmaster gave up his bed to him, and it was decided, should the patient not be better by the morrow, to send to C. for the apothecary.

Next day the hussar was worse. His servant rode to the neighbouring town for the apothecary. Dunya laid a handkerchief soaked in vinegar round his head, and sat beside his bed with her sewing. In the postmaster's presence the patient moaned and could scarcely utter a word, though he drank two cups of coffee and moaned out an order for dinner. Dunya never left his side. He constantly begged for a drink, and Dunya as constantly brought him a mug of the lemonade she had prepared with her own hands. The patient moistened his lips, and every time he returned the mug he pressed Dunya's hand in his feeble grasp, by way of showing his gratitude. The apothecary arrived at dinner-time. He felt the patient's pulse, spoke to him in German, and declared, in Russian, that all he needed was rest, and that he would be able to resume his journey in a couple of days. The hussar handed him twenty-five rubles in payment for his visit, and invited him to dinner. The apothecary accepted the invitation and the two of them ate heartily, drank the contents of a bottle of wine, and were vastly pleased with each other.

Another day passed and the hussar recovered completely. He was extremely gay, joking incessantly, now with Dunya, now with the postmaster, whistling tunes, chatting with travellers, entering their relays in the ledger, and making the kindly postmaster so fond of him that by the morning of the third day he could hardly bear to part with his pleasant lodger. It was a Sunday, and Dunya got ready to go to church. The hussar's sleigh was brought round. He bade the post-

master farewell, rewarding him generously for his board and lodging. He said good-bye to Dunya, too, offering to drive her as far as the church, which was at the other end of the village. Dunya seemed perplexed.... "What are you afraid of?" her father said. "His Honour isn't a wolf—he won't bite you; let him drive you to the church." Dunya got into the sleigh and sat down next to the hussar, the servant leaped on to the box-seat, the driver whistled, and the horses galloped off.

The unfortunate postmaster could never understand how it was that he had allowed his Dunya to go with the hussar, how he could have been so blind, what could have possessed him! Hardly half an hour passed when he began to feel a gnawing at his heart, and was overcome by anxiety to such an extent that he could no longer contain himself, and went to the church to look for her. As he approached it he saw the people already coming out, but Dunya was neither in the churchyard, nor in the porch. He hastened into the church; the priest had left the altar, the sexton was extinguishing the candles, two old women were still saying their prayers in a corner; but there was no Dunya to be seen. The unhappy father forced himself to ask the sexton if she had been at the service. The sexton replied that she had not. The postmaster returned home more dead than alive. He had only one hope left—Dunya with the levity of youth might have gone on to the next posting station, where her godmother lived. He awaited the return of the horses which he had sent with the carriage in an agony of impatience. But the day passed, and the driver did not come back. At last, towards night, he rode up alone, tipsy, and the bearer of appalling tidings: "Dunya had gone on from the next posting station with the hussar."

The old man never got over his misfortune, and that evening took to his bed—the very bed on which the youthful impostor had lain the day before. The postmaster, reviewing all the circumstances, now guessed that the young man's illness had been feigned. The poor old man was seized with a raging fever and was taken to C., another postmaster being temporarily appointed in his place. He was attended by the very same doctor who had visited the hussar and who now assured the postmaster that the young man had been perfectly well, and that he had guessed his evil intentions at the time, but had said nothing, for fear of the hussar's whip. Whether the German spoke the truth, or merely wished to show off his perspicacity, he did not afford his unhappy patient the least consolation. The postmaster had hardly recovered from his illness when he asked the authorities at C. for two months' leave, and, without a word of his intentions to anyone, set off on foot to look for his daughter. From the ledger he discovered that Captain Minsky had travelled from Smolensk to Petersburg. The coachman who drove him said that Dunya had wept all the way, although apparently going of her own free will. "God willing," thought the postmaster, "I shall bring my strayed lamb home." Inspired by this thought he arrived in Petersburg, putting up at the barracks of the Izmailov Regiment, in the house of a retired non-commissioned officer, and old comrade-in-arms of his from the days of his military service. And from there he began his search. He quickly discovered that Captain Minsky was in Petersburg, living at the Demutov tavern. The postmaster determined to see him.

Early in the morning he arrived at the hussar's front door and requested the servant to inform his honour that an old soldier wished to see him. The servant, polishing a riding-boot on a boot-tree, told him that his gentleman was asleep, and did not receive anyone before eleven o'clock. The postmaster went away and returned at the appointed hour. Minsky himself came out to him in his dressing-gown and a crimson fez. "What can I do for you, brother?" he asked. The old man's heart seethed with emotion, tears welled up in his eyes, and he could only mutter, in trembling accents: "Your Honour! For God's sake, Your Honour. . . ." Minsky cast a rapid glance at him, flushed crimson, took him by the hand, led him to his study, and locked the door from the inside. "Your Honour," went on the old man. "What is lost is gone forever, but give me back my poor Dunya! You have had your joy of her—do not ruin her for naught." "What has been done cannot be undone," said the young man, who was evidently quite overcome. "I have wronged you and am willing to ask your forgiveness. But you must not think me capable of deserting Dunya. She will be happy, I give you my word of honour. What do you want with her? She loves me, she has become unused to her former condition. Neither you nor she could ever forget what has happened." Then, thrusting something into the postmaster's cuff, he unlocked the door and the old man, hardly knowing how, found himself in the street.

He stood motionless for a long time, and at last noticed that there was a bundle of paper beneath his cuff. He drew it out, and unfolded a number of crumpled five- and ten-ruble notes. Tears welled up afresh in his eyes, tears of indignation. He crumpled the notes into a ball, flung them on the ground, trampled them beneath his heel, and went away. . . . After walking a few yards he stood still, bethought himself and . . . retraced his steps. But the notes were no longer there. A well-dressed young man, on seeing him, ran up to a *droshky*, and got in hastily, shouting: "Drive on!" The postmaster made no attempt to pursue him. He decided to go back to his posting station, but first wanted to see his poor Dunya, if only once. And so, two days later, he went to Minsky's quarters again. But the military servant told him sternly that his gentleman received no one, shouldered him out of the hall, and slammed the door in his face. The postmaster stood outside for some time—and then he went away.

That same evening he was walking along Liteinaya Street, having attended a service at the Church of All Martyrs. An elegant carriage dashed past him, and the postmaster recognized Minsky. The carriage stopped in front of a three-storey house, drawing up at the door, and the hussar leaped into the porch. A happy thought passed through the postmaster's mind. Turning back till he got to the carriage, he asked the coachman: "Whose horse is this, brother? Not Minsky's?" "Yes, it is," said the coachman. "Why do you ask?" "I'll tell you why—your master told me to take a note to his Dunya, and I've forgotten where she lives, this Dunya." "Why she lives here, on the next floor. But you're late with your note, brother. He's with her himself, now." "No matter," said the postmaster, with a strange fluttering at his heart. "Thanks for putting me right, but I must keep my promise." And with these words he mounted the steps.

The door was locked. He rang the bell and passed a few seconds in an agony of suspense. The key rattled in the lock and the door was opened. "Does Avdotya Samsonovna live here?" he asked. "Yes," replied the young maidservant. "What do you want with her?" Without replying the postmaster entered the hall. "You can't go in!" the servant called

after him. "Avdotya Samsonovna has company." But the postmaster, taking no notice, walked on. The two first rooms he passed through were in darkness, but there was a light in the third. He made for the open door and came to a stop. Minsky was seated deep in thought in the splendidly furnished room. Dunya, attired in the height of fashion, was perched on the arm of his chair, as if riding side-saddle in the English manner. She was gazing tenderly at Minsky, twisting his black curls round her fingers, which gleamed with jewels. Poor postmaster! Never had his daughter seemed lovelier to him; he watched her with involuntary admiration. "Who's there?" she cried, without raising her head. He stood silent. Not receiving an answer, Dunya looked up ... and fell on the carpet with a shriek. Minsky, alarmed, rushed to pick her up, but catching sight of the old postmaster at the door, left Dunya and approached him, shaking with rage. "What do you want?" he said through clenched teeth. "Why do you follow me about like a thief? Are you after my life? Get out!" And seizing the old man by the collar of his coat with his strong hand, he shoved him out on to the stairs.

The old man went back to his lodging. His friend advised him to lodge a complaint, but the postmaster, after thinking it over, dismissed the idea with a wave of his hand, and decided to leave things as they were. Two days later he left Petersburg and went back to his posting station, where he resumed his former work. "And it is now almost three years," he said in conclusion, "since I have been living without Dunya, with never a word of her. Whether she is alive or dead God alone knows. Anything is possible. She is not the first and will not be the last to be seduced by a passing fop, to be first kept by him, and then abandoned.

There are plenty of young fools like her in Petersburg, to-day dressed up in satin and velvet, and to-morrow, look you, sweeping the crossings with the riff-raff. Sometimes when I think Dunya may be languishing there, I can't help the sinful wish that she were in her grave. . . ."

Such was the tale of my friend the old postmaster, a tale constantly interrupted by tears, which he wiped away picturesquely with the hem of his coat, like the zealous Terentyich[12] in the exquisite ballad of Dmitriev. These tears were partially called forth by the punch, of which he imbibed five glasses in the course of his narrative, but they nevertheless moved me powerfully. After I took my leave of him it was long before I could get the thought of the old postmaster out of my head, or stop thinking of the unfortunate Dunya.

Not so long ago, passing through the hamlet of X., I remembered my old friend. I learned that the posting station which he had ruled over no longer existed. No one could give me a satisfactory answer to the question: "Is the old postmaster still alive?" I felt a desire to visit the familiar parts, and hiring horses drove to the village of N.

It was autumn. The sky was covered with grey clouds, a cold wind was blowing from the empty cornfields, bearing red and yellow leaves from the trees in its passage. I arrived at the village just before sunset, and stopped in front of the postmaster's house. A stout woman came out into the porch (where poor Dunya had once kissed me), and replied to my inquiries that the old postmaster had been dead a year, that his house now belonged to a brewer and that she herself was the brewer's wife. I began to regret my useless journey and the seven rubles expended in vain. "What did

he die of?" I asked the brewer's wife. "He drank himself to death, Sir," quoth she. "And where is he buried?" "Just beyond the village, beside his late wife." "Couldn't someone take me to his grave?" "Why, certainly. Hi, Vanka! Let that cat alone! Take the gentleman to the cemetery and show him the postmaster's grave."

A ragged urchin, red-haired and one-eyed, ran up and led me to the end of the village.

"Did you know the postmaster?" I asked him on the way.

"Oh, yes, I knew him! He taught me to make whistles. When he came out of the tavern (God rest his soul!) we used to run after him and say: 'Uncle! Uncle! Give us some nuts!' And he would give us all nuts. He was always playing with us."

"And do travellers ever ask after him?"

"There aren't many travellers any more. Unless it's some assize-judge and he never thinks about dead people. But there was a lady this summer, she asked about the old postmaster and went to see his grave."

"What sort of lady?" I asked inquisitively.

"A lovely lady," said the boy. "She was in a coach-and-six, with three children and a nurse, and a black pug. And when they told her the old postmaster was dead, she cried, and said to the children: 'You stay here quietly, while I go to the cemetery.' I offered to take her there. But the lady said: 'I know the way myself.' And she gave me a silver five-kopek piece—such a kind lady!"

We arrived at the cemetery, a bleak spot with no railings, dotted with wooden crosses, and quite unprotected from the sun's rays. Never in my life have I seen such a melancholy cemetery.

"This is the grave of the old postmaster," said the little boy, leaping on to a mound of sand in which a black cross bearing a brass icon had been stuck.

"And did the lady come here?" I asked.

"She did," replied Vanya. "I watched her from the distance. She lay here, a long time she lay. And then she went to the village, the lady, and called for the priest, and gave him some money and went away and me she gave a silver five-kopek piece—a very nice lady!"

I, too, gave the small boy a five-kopek piece, and did not regret either my journey or the seven rubles it had cost me.

Lady
into
Lassie

In any attire, sweetheart, you are charming.

BOGDANOVICH[13]

THE ESTATE of Ivan Petrovich Berestov was situated in one of our remotest provinces. Ivan Petrovich served in the Guard in his youth, obtained his discharge in the year 1797 and went to live on his property, never again to leave it. He married a poor gentlewoman who died in child-birth during his absence some distance away on a hunting-expedition. He soon found consolation for his loss in the management of his property. He had his house built according to plans drawn up by himself, set up a cloth-factory on the estate, increased his income, and regarded himself as the wisest man in the whole district, which opinion his neighbours, who got into the habit of paying him long visits with their families and their hunting-dogs, did nothing to shake. On weekdays he went about in a velveteen jacket, on holidays he donned a frock-coat of homespun cloth; he kept all the accounts himself, and read nothing but the Proceedings of the Senate. On the whole he was well-liked, though considered proud. His nearest neighbour, Grigori Ivanovich Muromsky, was the only person who did not get on with him. And he was a Russian gentleman of the old school. Having frittered away the greater part of his property in Moscow, and become a widower, he went to live in the sole village remaining to him, and there continued to waste his substance, but this time in a different manner. He laid out a garden in the English style, on which he expended almost all the money he had. His stable-boys were attired as English jockeys. His daughter had an English governess. He farmed his land according to the English system.

But alien ways do not suit Russian corn,

and despite considerable diminution of expenditure, the income of Grigori Ivanovich did not increase; even in the country he found ways of accumulating fresh debts; and with it all he was accounted an able man, being the first landowner to think of mortgaging his estate with the Court of Chancery—a manoeuvre in those days considered extremely complicated and audacious. Among those who censured him, his sternest critic was Berestov, whose chief characteristic was a dislike of innovations. He was unable to speak calmly of his neighbour's Anglomania, and never tired of finding fault with him. When showing visitors over his estate he would reply to their praises of his management with sly irony: "Well, well! We don't do things here the way neighbour Grigori Ivanovich does. It's not for us to ruin ourselves in the English style. We are thankful if we get enough to eat, the

Russian way!" Thanks to the zeal of the neighbours, these and other quips, which you may be sure lost nothing in the telling, were brought to the ears of Grigori Ivanovich. The Anglomaniac was no more able to bear criticism than are our journalists. Infuriated, he dubbed the rural Zoilus a bear and a provincial.

Such were the relations between these two proprietors when Berestov's son came to visit him. Educated at the university of X., he intended to go into the army, but his father would not give his consent to this. The young man felt himself to be completely unfitted for government service. Neither would give in, and in the meantime the youthful Alexei lived the life of a gentleman at large, cultivating a moustache so as to be ready for any exigency.

Alexei was indeed a fine young fellow. It certainly would be a pity if his graceful figure were destined never to be enclosed in a military uniform, and if, instead of cutting a figure as a dashing horseman, he would have to spend his youth stooping over official documents. When the neighbours saw him at the hunt, always galloping in the forefront, regardless of obstacles in his way, they agreed unanimously that he would never make a good government official. Glances full of interest, which not seldom grew to admiration, were cast at him by the young ladies in the neighbourhood; but Alexei took very little notice of them, so that they felt bound to ascribe his coldness to a love affair. By way of corroboration of this view a paper was passed from hand to hand, bearing a copy of an address from one of his letters: *Akulina Petrovna Kurochkina, Moscow, opposite the Monastery of St. Alexis, at the house of the copper-smith Savelyev, you are kindly requested to hand this letter to A.N.R.*

Those of my readers who have never lived in the country can have no idea how delightful these provincial young ladies are. Brought up in the fresh air, in the shade of their apple-orchards, they derive all their knowledge of life and society from books. Solitude, liberty and reading early develop in them emotions and passions unknown to our pampered beauties. For these country maidens the jingle of bells is an adventure, a visit to the nearest town a momentous event in their lives, and visitors leave lasting, sometimes lifelong memories behind them. Anybody is entitled, of course, to laugh at certain oddities which may characterize these young ladies; but the jests of a superficial observer cannot destroy their essential qualities, of which the principal one is distinction of character, that *individualité* without which, according to Jean-Paul Richter, no human being can be great. It may be that in the great capitals women receive a superior education; but the ways of society soon exercise their levelling influence on character, and make the minds of women as alike as their head-gear. This is said neither in judgement nor censure, but nevertheless *nota nostra manet,** as an old writer has it.

It is easy to conceive the impression bound to be made on our young ladies by Alexei. He was the first gloomy, disillusionized being they had met, the first to speak to them of spent pleasures and blighted youth; and to crown all he wore a black ring set with a death's head. All this was quite new to the province. All the girls were frantic about him.

But none of them devoted so much thought to him as the daughter of the Anglomaniac, Lisa (or Betsy, as her father

* The observation rests.

usually called her). The fathers did not visit each other's houses, so that she had not yet seen Alexei, whereas all the young women of the neighbourhood talked of nothing but him. Lisa was seventeen years old. Her attractive, olive-skinned countenance was lit up by a pair of black eyes. Being an only child, she was, of course, spoilt and petted. Her liveliness and incessant pranks were the delight of her father and the despair of her governess, Miss Jackson, a starched spinster of forty, who enamelled her cheeks and dyed her eyebrows, read *Pamela* right through every six months, for all of which she received two thousand rubles a year, and nearly died of boredom in this *barbarous land of Russia.*

Lisa was attended by her maid Nastya, who was a little older, but just as flighty as her young mistress. Lisa was very fond of her, let her into all her secrets, and enlisted her aid in the preparation of her pranks. In short, Nastya was a much more important personage in the village of Priluchino than many a *confidente* in a French tragedy.

"May I go out visiting to-day?" asked Nastya while dressing her mistress one morning.

"Certainly! Where are you going?"

"To Tugilovo, to the Berestovs'. It's the name-day of their cook's wife, and she came yesterday to invite us to dinner."

"Oh, indeed!" said Lisa. "The masters are at odds, but the servants entertain one another!"

"Our masters' quarrels are no business of ours," retorted Nastya. "Besides, I'm *your* servant, not your Papa's. You and young Berestov have not quarrelled yet, you know, so let the old folk fight it out among themselves!"

"Try and get a sight of Alexei Berestov, Nastya, and tell me exactly what he's like and what sort of person he is."

Nastya promised, and Lisa waited impatiently all day for her maid's return. Nastya came back in the evening. "Well, Lisaveta Grigoryevna," she said, as soon as she got into the room. "I've seen young Berestov; I had a good look at him. We were together all day."

"What? Tell me, tell me everything right from the beginning!"

"Certainly. We all got there, I, Anisya Yegorovna, Nenila, Dunya. . . ."

"Never mind all that! Well, and then?"

"Let me tell you everything from the very beginning. So we got there just at dinner-time. The room was full of people. The servants of the Kolbins and the Zakharyevs were there, the steward's wife and daughters, the Khlupin servants. . . ."

"Tell me about Berestov!"

"Wait a minute. So we sat down to table, the steward's wife next to the hostess, I next to her . . . the daughters pouted, but what do I care about them?"

"Oh, Nastya, how tiresome you are with your everlasting details!"

"And how impatient you are! Well, so we got up from table . . . the dinner lasted three hours, very good it was— there were blue, red, and stripy *blanc-manger* tarts. . . . So we got up, and went to play catch in the garden, and the young master came there."

"Well? Is it true he's so good-looking?"

"He's ever so good-looking, really handsome. Slim, tall, red-cheeked. . . ."

"Really! And I was sure he would be pale. Well? How did he strike you—mournful, pensive?"

"Not a bit of it! I never saw such a mad fellow in my life. He took it into his head to play catch with us."

"*He* play catch with you! You don't mean it!"

"But he did! And what's more—whenever he caught anyone he gave her a kiss."

"Oh, Nastya, you're telling stories!"

"I'm not then! I could hardly get away from him. He stayed with us the whole day."

"But everyone says he's in love, and never looks at anyone."

"That's as it may be, he certainly looked at me and at Tanya, the steward's daughter. And he didn't overlook the Kolbins Pasha—come to think of it, he didn't overlook any of us, the scamp!"

"Astonishing! Well, and what do they say about him in the house?"

"They say he's a very nice gentleman, ever so kind and cheery. The only thing wrong with him is that he's too fond of running after the girls. But I don't see much harm in that myself—he'll get over it."

"How I should like to see him!" sighed Lisa.

"Well, that's easy enough. Tugilovo isn't far from us—only three versts. Take a walk over there, or go on horseback, you're sure to meet him. He goes out every morning early, with his gun."

"Oh, that would never do! He might think I was running after him. Besides, our fathers are on bad terms, so I can't get to know him anyhow. . . . Oh, Nastya! I'll tell you what! I'll dress myself as a peasant girl!"

"Do that! Put on a homespun blouse, and a *sarafan*, and walk boldly over to Tugilovo. I vouch for it Berestov won't overlook you!"

"And I can talk just like the village people. Oh, Nastya, dear Nastya! What a splendid idea!" And Lisa went to bed with the firm intention of carrying her entertaining scheme out. The next day she went to work on its execution, sending to the market for thick homespun, blue print and brass buttons. With Nastya's aid she cut out a blouse and a *sarafan*, and set all the servant-girls to work on it, so that by evening everything was ready. Lisa tried on her new attire and, looking at herself in the mirror, could not but own that she had never seen herself so pretty. To rehearse her part, she bowed low and walked about, tossing her head from side to side like one of those clay cats whose heads move in a socket, spoke in the local dialect, covering her mouth with her sleeve when she laughed, and earned the full approval of Nastya. The only difficulty arose when she tried walking about the yard barefoot, for the sods hurt her tender feet, and the sand and gravel pricked her intolerably. Here, too, Nastya came to her aid. She took the measure of Lisa's foot, and ran into the fields to find the shepherd Trofim, from whom she ordered a pair of bast shoes. Lisa was awake the next day before daybreak, while the rest of the household was still sleeping. Nastya stood waiting at the gate for the shepherd to pass. The horn sounded and the village herds wound their way past the landowner's house. As he went by, Trofim handed Nastya a pair of small, brightly coloured slippers, for which he received fifty kopeks from her in payment. Lisa slid noiselessly into her peasant attire, gave Nastya whispered instructions with regard to Miss Jackson, left the house by the back-porch and ran through the kitchen-garden into the open fields.

Dawn was brightening the eastern sky, and the clouds seemed to be drawn up in golden ranks, awaiting the sun, like courtiers awaiting the appearance of their tsar; the transparent sky, the morning freshness, the dew, the breeze and the singing of birds filled Lisa's heart with childish gaiety; in her fear of encountering someone she knew she seemed to fly rather than walk. When she arrived at the copse which marked the limits of her father's property, she slowed down. It was here that she was to wait for Alexei. Her heart beat violently—why, she could not have said; but it is the trepidation accompanying our youthful ventures which constitutes their principal charm. Lisa entered the twilight of the copse. Muffled sounds greeted the girl's ears from its depths, and her gaiety was instantly subdued. Little by little she gave herself up to blissful meditations. She thought ... but who can say exactly what a girl of seventeen thinks about in a copse, between five and six o'clock of a spring morning? She walked on, absorbed in her thoughts, along a pathway shaded on either hand by tall trees, when suddenly a fine pointer ran barking towards her. Lisa cried out in alarm. Almost at the same moment a voice was heard, exclaiming: *"Tout beau Sbogar, ici!"* and a young huntsman appeared from behind some bushes. "Don't be afraid, pretty one!" he said to Lisa. "My dog doesn't bite." Lisa, who had quite recovered from her fright, was quick to take advantage of the situation. "But I *am* afraid, Sir," she said, feigning a mixture of fear and shyness. "Look how fierce he is! He'll jump on me again." Alexei (the reader will have guessed the stranger's identity), gazed steadily the while at the peasant lass. "I'll go with you if you're afraid," he said. "Will you allow me to walk beside you?" "Who's to prevent you?" returned Lisa. "Anyone is free to use the road." "Where do you come from?" "From

Priluchino. I'm the daughter of Vasili, the blacksmith. I've come to gather mushrooms." (Lisa dangled a bark basket from a string.) "And who are you, Sir? From Tugilovo?" "Quite right," replied Alexei. "I'm the young master's valet." Alexei wished to meet her on an equal footing. But Lisa looked at him and laughed. "No, you're not," she said. "You can't take *me* in! I can see you're the master himself." "What makes you think so?" "Everything about you." "But tell me what!" "As if one couldn't tell the master from the man! You're dressed differently, you talk differently, and you don't call your dog the way we do." Lisa's charms grew upon Alexei. Accustomed to treat the pretty village girls with scant ceremony, he tried to put his arm round her; but Lisa sprang back and suddenly assumed an expression so cold and forbidding that Alexei, though amused, refrained from further advances. "If you want to be friends with me in future," she said primly, "you mustn't forget yourself." "Who taught you to talk like that?" asked Alexei, laughing heartily. "Was it my friend Nastenka, your young lady's serving-woman? Now we see how education is spread!" Lisa felt that she had been speaking out of character, and hastened to get back into her assumed role. "Well," she said, "do you suppose I never go to the big house? I see and hear all sorts of things there, you know! But I shan't get many mushrooms, standing here and chattering with you. You go your way, Sir, and I'll go mine. Good morning, Sir." Lisa made as if to go. Alexei seized her hand and held her back. "What's you name, pretty one?" "Akulina," replied Lisa, trying to extricate her fingers from Alexei's hand. "Let go of me, Sir—it's time for me to go home." "Well, friend Akulina, I shall certainly go and see your father, Vasili the blacksmith." "What?" cried Lisa. "For God's sake don't do that! If they were to find out at home that I had been talking to a gentleman all alone in the copse I should get it. My father, Vasili the blacksmith, would beat me black and blue." "But I must see you again." "I shall be coming here for mushrooms." "But when?" "I don't know—to-morrow perhaps!" "Akulina dear, I would kiss you, if I dared. Make it to-morrow, at the same time—do!" "Very well." "And you won't disappoint me?" "No, I won't." "Swear you won't!" "I swear by the Holy Cross that I'll come."

The young people parted. Lisa went out of the wood, crossed the field, crept into the garden, and rushed headlong to the farm-stead, where Nastya was waiting for her. Here she changed back into her own clothes, answering the eager questions of her *confidente* with an abstracted air, and hastened to make her appearance in the drawing-room. The table was laid, breakfast was ready, and Miss Jackson, powdered and wasp-waisted even at this early hour, was cutting bread into thin slices. Lisa's father praised her for being out so early. "There is nothing healthier," he observed, "than getting up at daybreak." He then cited several instances of longevity culled from English periodicals, remarking that all those who had lived to over a hundred had abstained from vodka, and got up at daybreak summer and winter. Lisa hardly heard what he said. She was mentally reviewing all the circumstances of the morning's rendezvous, the entire conversation between Akulina and the young hunter, and was beginning to feel qualms of conscience. She assured herself in vain that their conversation had not overstepped the limits of decency, that her prank could not possibly have any untoward consequences—conscience spoke louder than reason. The chief cause of her uneasiness was the promise she had given for the morrow, and she was within an ace of breaking her solemn vow. But Alexei, after waiting for her in vain, might go to the village to look for the true Akulina, the blacksmith's daughter, a plump pock-marked lass, and in this way guess at the trick Lisa had played him. The thought of this appalled her, and she made up her mind to go again to the copse the following morning, disguised as Akulina.

Alexei's ecstasy was unalloyed, all day he thought of nothing but his new acquaintance, and when night came his dreams were haunted by visions of the dusky beauty. He was up and dressed almost before the dawn. Without waiting to charge his musket he went out with his faithful Sbogar, and hastened to the place of the promised rendezvous. About half an hour passed in what was unbearable suspense for him; at last he caught sight of a blue *sarafan* flitting among the bushes, and rushed to meet his dear Akulina. She received his ecstatic gratitude with a smile, but Alexei was quick to note the traces of dejection and anxiety on her countenance. He inquired the reason for them. Lisa confessed to him that she now regarded her conduct as indiscreet, and repented it, that she had been unwilling to break her word this time, but that this would be their last meeting, and that she begged him to break off an acquaintance which could hold nothing good for them. Of course she expressed all this in country dialect, but thoughts and feelings so unusual in a simple girl astonished Alexei. He exerted all his eloquence to make Akulina retract her decision; he assured her of the innocence of his intentions, vowed never to give her grounds for repentance, to obey her will in all things, imploring her not to deprive him of the joy of meeting her alone, if only every other day, or two days a week. He employed the language of true passion, and, at the moment, really felt that he was in love. Lisa heard him out in silence. "Give me your word," she said, when he had finished, "that you will never look for me in the village, or make any inquiries about me. Give me your word never to seek a meeting with me, beyond those which I myself appoint." Alexei was about to promise "by the Holy Cross," but Lisa stopped him with a smile. "I don't ask for vows," she said. "Your word is enough for me." They then conversed in the friendliest fashion, walking about the wood side by side till the moment when Lisa said: "It is time for me to go." They parted and Alexei, left to himself, could not understand how it was that a simple village lass had been able to get such unmistakable power over him in a mere two meetings. His relations with Akulina held the charm of novelty for him, and though the edicts of the strange peasant girl appeared to him onerous, the thought of breaking his word never so much as entered his head. Truth to tell, Alexei, despite the sinister ring, the mysterious correspondence, and his air of disillusion, was just a good-hearted, impulsive youth, with an unspoilt heart, capable of enjoying the most innocent pleasures.

Had I no one but myself to please I should now embark upon a detailed description of the young people's trysts, of their ever-increasing mutual liking and confidence, their occupations, their talks; but I am aware that the majority of my readers would not share my enjoyment of this. Such details invariably appear insipid, and I will therefore omit them, merely remarking that before two months had passed, my Alexei was head over ears in love, and Lisa, though less articulate, was almost equally so. They both rejoiced in the present, and gave little thought to the future.

The thought of indissoluble bonds crossed their minds frequently, but they never spoke about this to each other. The reason is not far to seek—attached as Alexei was to his dear

Akulina, he fully realized the distance between himself and a poor peasant girl; and Lisa, knowing the hostility which existed between their fathers, did not dare to hope for a reconciliation between them. Moreover, her vanity was secretly tickled by an obscure romantic hope of at last seeing the heir to Tugilovo at the feet of the daughter of the Priluchino blacksmith. And then an important event bade fair to alter their standing in each other's eyes.

One fine cold morning (one of those mornings which are so frequent in our Russian autumn), Ivan Petrovich Berestov went out riding, taking with him, just in case anything should turn up, five or six greyhounds, his groom, and a few serf-boys with rattles. At the very same moment, Grigori Ivanovich Muromsky, tempted out by the fine weather, ordered his mare to be saddled, and trotted over his anglicized estate. As he rode up to the wood, he caught sight of his neighbour, proudly erect in the saddle, wearing a jacket lined with fox-fur, and awaiting the appearance of the hare which his lads were chasing with shouts and rattles out of the bushes. If Grigori Ivanovich could have foreseen this encounter he would undoubtedly have turned in another direction, but he came upon Berestov quite unexpectedly, and found himself within a pistol shot of him. There was no help for it. Muromsky, every inch the urbane European, rode up to his enemy and greeted him courteously. Berestov responded as cordially as a chained bear bidden by his leader to bow to the gentry. Just then the hare leaped out of the wood and made for the open field. Berestov and his groom hallooed at the top of their voices; they unleashed the dogs, and galloped after the hare at full speed. Muromsky's horse, which had never been used for hunting, took fright and bolted. Muromsky, who gave himself out for a fine horseman, let it have its head, secretly

pleased at the accident which had rid him of an unpleasant encounter. But his horse, galloping to the brink of a gully which it had not seen till then, suddenly shied, and Muromsky was unable to keep his seat. Falling rather heavily on the frost-hardened earth, he lay there, cursing his dock-tailed mare, which, as if coming to her senses, halted as soon as she felt herself to be riderless. Ivan Petrovich galloped up and asked Grigori Ivanovich if he had hurt himself. In the meantime the groom had brought back the culprit, and stood holding her by the bridle. He assisted Muromsky to mount, and Berestov invited the latter to his house. Muromsky felt obliged to accept the invitation, and thus Berestov returned in triumph, having caught a hare and led his enemy home, wounded and almost a prisoner of war.

The neighbours conversed in a perfectly friendly manner over their breakfast. Muromsky asked Berestov to let him have a carriage, admitting that the shaking-up he had received had unfitted him to ride his mare back. Berestov accompanied him to the entrance and Muromsky did not leave until he had received Berestov's word of honour to bring Alexei Ivanovich to take pot-luck with him the very next day. Thus it happened that the old, deep-rooted enmity showed promise of coming to an end, through the timidity of a dock-tailed mare.

Lisa came running out to meet Grigori Ivanovich. "What's the matter, Papa?" she cried in astonishment. "Why are you limping? Where's your horse? Whose carriage is that?" "You'll never guess, *my dear*," replied Grigori Ivanovich, who was fond of using English forms of address. He gave her an account of the whole incident. Lisa could not believe her ears. Grigori Ivanovich, giving her no time to recover from her astonishment, told her that the two Berestovs were coming to take dinner with them the next day. "What!" she exclaimed, turning pale. "The Berestovs—father and son? Dining with us to-morrow! You can do as you like, Papa, but *I* shall certainly not appear." "Are you mad?" exclaimed her father. "What makes you so shy all of a sudden? Or is it that you feel a hereditary hatred for him, like the heroine of a novel? I won't have any more of this fooling. . . ." "No, Papa, not for the world, not for anything in the world, will I appear in front of the Berestovs!" Grigori Ivanovich, who knew full well that there was nothing to be gained by opposing her, shrugged his shoulders, gave up the argument, and betook himself to rest after his memorable ride.

Lisaveta Grigoryevna went to her room and called Nastya to her. The two held a lengthy conference on the subject of the morrow's visit. What would Alexei think when he recognized in the well-bred young lady his own Akulina? What would be his opinion of her conduct, her principles, her prudence? At the same time Lisa was extremely anxious to see the impression made on him by so unexpected a meeting. . . . Suddenly she had a bright idea. She instantly communicated it to Nastya. Both were delighted with it and determined to put it into practice at all costs.

The next day at breakfast Grigori Ivanovich asked his daughter if she still intended to hide from the Berestovs. "Since you wish it I will receive them, Papa," replied Lisa, "but only on condition that, whatever the guise in which I appear before them, and whatever I do, you will not scold me and will not show the slightest sign of astonishment or dissatisfaction." "Up to your tricks again!" said Grigori Ivanovich, laughing. "Very well, I agree. Have your own way, my black-eyed madcap!" With these words he imprinted a kiss on her brow, and Lisa ran off to make her preparations.

Punctually at two a home-built carriage drawn by six horses entered the drive, rolling past the circle of bright green turf. Berestov senior, supported by two of Muromsky's liveried footmen, mounted the steps of the porch. His son came in his wake on horseback, and accompanied him to the dining-room, where the table was laid in readiness. Muromsky received his guests with the utmost cordiality, inviting them to inspect his garden and menageries before dinner, and leading them along well-swept gravel paths. Old Berestov secretly deplored the time and labour wasted on such useless whims, but kept silent from courtesy. His son shared neither the disapproval of the thrifty landowner, nor the enthusiasm of the complacent Anglomaniac. He was waiting impatiently for the appearance of the host's daughter, of whom he had heard much, and although his feelings were, as we know, engaged, a beautiful young woman was always sure of stirring his imagination.

The three of them returned to the drawing-room and sat down. The old men recalled former times and exchanged stories of military life, and Alexei busied himself with thinking of the part he should play in the presence of Lisa. He decided that an air of cold *hauteur* would be the most appropriate, and prepared himself accordingly. The door opened; he turned his head with an indifference and elaborate scorn, calculated to make the heart of the most hardened coquette throb. Unfortunately it was not Lisa, but Miss Jackson, powdered, corsetted, her eyes lowered, who entered the room dropping a curtsey, so that Alexei's grand military manoeuvre was quite lost. Hardly had he time to recover his senses, when the door again opened, and this time Lisa came into the room. All rose: the father was just going to introduce the guests, when he stopped short and hastily bit his lip. . . . Lisa, his dusky Lisa, was powdered to the ears, tricked out to rival Miss Jackson; false curls, much fairer than her own hair, were frizzed like the wig of Louis Quatorze; sleeves *à l'imbécile* stuck out like Madame Pompadour's farthingale; she was laced in till her figure was like the letter X, and all her mother's diamonds which had not yet been pawned blazed at her fingers, her throat, and her ears. Alexei could not possibly have recognized his Akulina in this brilliant, but ludicrous female. His father rose to kiss her hand, and Alexei unwillingly followed his example. As his lips brushed her slender fingers it seemed to him he noticed a slight tremor pass over them. At the same moment he caught sight of a little foot, obviously advanced with the purpose of showing off the extravagantly coquettish shoe. This reconciled him somewhat to the rest of her attire. As for the powder and paint, it must be admitted that in the simplicity of his heart he did not at first notice them, and even later he did not suspect them. Grigori Ivanovich remembered his promise and endeavoured to evince not the slightest astonishment. But his daughter's whim amused him mightily, and he could hardly keep a straight face. But it was no laughing matter for the prudish Englishwoman. She guessed at once that the paint and powder had been filched from her dressing table, and a crimson flush of vexation showed beneath the artificial pallor of her cheeks. She cast furious glances at the youthful miscreant who, postponing explanations to some future date, pretended not to notice them.

They took their seats at the table. Alexei continued in his role of an absent-minded, pensive individual; Lisa simpered, speaking through her teeth in a sing-song voice, and only in French. Her father kept looking at her, ignorant of her purpose, but finding it all extremely amusing. The Englishwoman was reduced to speechless fury. The only person who felt at ease was Ivan Petrovich, who ate for two, drank his usual fill, laughed at his own jokes, and conversed with ever-increasing friendliness.

At last the time came to leave the table. The guests took their departure, and Grigori Ivanovich was free to indulge in laughter and questions. "What put it into your head to fool them?" he asked Lisa. "And by the way, powder suits you! I don't understand the secrets of a lady's toilet, but if I were you I'd start using powder. Not too much, of course, just a little." Lisa was charmed with the success of her idea. She flung her arms round her father's neck, promised to think over his advice, and ran off to propitiate the infuriated Miss Jackson, who could hardly be brought to open her door and listen to Lisa's excuses. Lisa told her she had been ashamed to show herself before strangers with her dark skin; she had not ventured to ask . . . she was sure dear, good Miss Jackson would forgive her . . . and so on, and so on. Miss Jackson, when convinced that Lisa had not meant to make fun of her, calmed down, kissed Lisa, bestowing upon her as a token of reconciliation a jar of English whitening, which Lisa received with every sign of sincere gratitude.

The reader will easily surmise that Lisa did not fail to appear at the trysting-place on the following day. "You went to see our gentlefolk yesterday," she said the moment she met Alexei. "What do you think of our young lady?" Alexei replied that he had not noticed her. "A pity!" ejaculated Lisa. "Why?" asked Alexei. "Because I wanted to ask you if it's true what they say. . ." "What do they say?" ". . .if it's true what they say . . . that I'm like her." "What nonsense! She's a fright compared to you!" "Oh, Sir, you shouldn't say that; our young lady is so fair, so elegant! How can I be compared with her!" Alexei vowed that she was better than all the fair young ladies in the world, and in order to allay her doubts entirely, proceeded to describe her mistress in such comic detail that Lisa laughed heartily. "And yet," she sighed, "my young lady may be ridiculous, but I am a mere unlettered dunce compared to her." "Eh," cried Alexei, "is that what worries you? If you like I'll start giving you lessons this very minute." "And why not?" exclaimed Lisa. "Why shouldn't I try?" "Do, my dear; let us start here and now." They sat down. Alexei produced a pencil and note-book from his pocket and Akulina learned the alphabet in a remarkably short time. Alexei could not contain his astonishment at her quickness. The next morning she wanted to try writing; at first the pencil would not obey her, but in a few minutes she was writing the letters quite well. "It's a marvel," said Alexei. "Why we're getting on faster than they're supposed to under the Lancaster system!" Indeed, by the third lesson Akulina was able to spell out *Natalya, Daughter of the Boyar*, interrupting her reading with remarks which amazed Alexei, and blotting a sheet with aphorisms copied from the same novel.

A week passed, and they were exchanging letters. Their post-office was a hollow in an ancient oak-tree. Nastya secretly fulfilled the function of postman. Alexei brought to the oak-tree letters written in a bold hand, and found there missives on cheap blue paper, scrawled over by his beloved. Akulina's style improved with every letter, and her mind formed and developed noticeably.

In the meantime the relations which had so lately sprung up between Ivan Petrovich Berestov and Grigori Ivanovich Muromsky were steadily improving, and soon turned into friendship, thanks to the following circumstances: Muromsky often reflected that at the death of Ivan Petrovich all his property would go to Alexei Ivanovich, when the latter would become one of the wealthiest proprietors in the district, and that there was no reason whatever why he should not marry Lisa. Old Berestov, for his part, while noting in his neighbour certain eccentricities (or, to borrow his own expression, a craze for everything English), did not, however, deny that he had many excellent qualities, among which unusual ingenuity was to be counted. Grigori Ivanovich was closely related to Count Pronsky, a distinguished and powerful man. The count might be of great use to Alexei, and Muromsky (thought Ivan Petrovich) would doubtless be glad of a chance to marry off his daughter advantageously. For some time the two old men kept their thoughts to themselves, but there came a day when they at last opened their hearts to each other and embraced, promising to look into the matter thoroughly. Each set about it in his own way. Muromsky foresaw a difficulty—namely, the bringing together of his Betsy and Alexei, whom she had not seen since the memorable dinner. It appeared that they were not greatly drawn to each other. At any rate, Alexei did not come to Priluchino again, and Lisa retired to her chamber whenever Ivan Petrovich honoured them with a visit. But Grigori Ivanovich said to himself, "If Alexei comes every day Betsy is bound to fall in love with him. It is in the nature of things. Time will settle everything."

Ivan Petrovich felt less uncertainty as to the success of his plans. That very evening he called his son into his study, lit his pipe, and said, after a short pause: "How is it, Alyosha, that you have quite stopped talking about a military career? Don't you sigh for a hussar's uniform any more?" "No, Sir," replied Alexei respectfully. "I see it is not to your liking that I should enter the hussars—it is my duty to submit to your wishes." "Good," said Ivan Petrovich. "You are a dutiful son, I see. That is a great consolation to me. And I, too, have no desire to force you. I shall not compel you to enter the government service—at present. And in the meanwhile I intend you to get married."

"Whom do you wish me to marry, Sir?" inquired the astonished Alexei.

"Lisaveta Grigoryevna Muromskaya," replied Ivan Petrovich. "Not a bad choice, I think."

"But, Sir, I am not thinking of marriage as yet."

"You are not thinking, and therefore I have thought for you, and made up my mind."

"But, Sir, I don't like Lisa Muromskaya."

"You'll like her afterwards. Love follows on habit."

"I do not feel myself capable of making her happy."

"Never mind her happiness. What? Is this your respect for your parent's wishes? For shame!"

"Like it or not, Sir, I do not wish to marry, and I will not do so."

"Either you get married, or I will curse you and, as God is my judge, I will sell the property and fritter away the price I get for it, without leaving you a kopek. I give you three days for reflection, and till then keep out of my sight!"

Alexei knew that if his father got an idea in his head there was no getting it out, not even, as Taras Skotinin[14] put it, "with a nail." But Alexei took after his sire, and it was just as difficult to get him to change his mind. He went to his room and pondered over the limits of parental authority, the personality of Lisaveta Grigoryevna, his father's solemn threat of making him a beggar, until finally his thoughts came to rest on Akulina. For the first time he became clearly aware that he was passionately in love with her. The romantic idea

of marrying a peasant girl and living by his own labours passed through his mind, and the more he thought about this determined act, the more reasonable did it seem. The trysts in the copse had ceased for some time on account of rainy weather. He sent Akulina a letter in which the writing was a model of clarity and the style frenzied, informing her of the imminent threat to their happiness and at the same time offering her his hand. He took the letter at once to the post-office in the hollow oak, and went to bed well satisfied with himself.

The next day, firm in his resolution, Alexei went early in the morning to see Muromsky, and speak frankly to him. He hoped to arouse his magnanimity and get him on his side. "Is Grigori Ivanovich at home?" he asked, reining in his horse in front of the porch of the Priluchino mansion. "No, Sir," replied the servant. "Grigori Ivanovich went away early this morning." "How vexatious!" he thought. "Well, is Lisaveta Grigoryevna at home?" "Yes, Sir." Alexei jumped off his horse, handing the reins to the servant, and went in unannounced.

"Everything will be settled," he said to himself, going towards the drawing-room. "I'll have a talk with the lady herself." He entered the room, and was thunderstruck. Lisa . . . no, Akulina, dear, olive-skinned Akulina, not in her *sarafan*, but in a white morning-gown, was sitting at the window reading his letter; she was so absorbed that she did not hear him come in. Alexei could not stifle a joyful exclamation. Lisa started, raised her head, cried out, and tried to run away. He tried to hold her back by force. "Akulina! Akulina!" Lisa tried to get away from him.... *"Mais laissez-moi donc, Monsieur! Mais êtes-vous fou?"* she kept saying, in the midst of her struggles. "Akulina! Akulina, my beloved!" he repeated over and over again, showering kisses on her hands. Miss Jackson, who was a witness of this scene, knew not what to think. Just then the door opened, and Grigori Ivanovich entered.

"Aha!" he cried. "I see you've taken things into your own hands. . . ."

The reader will relieve me of the superfluous task of describing the end of the story.

1830

NOTES

[1] A comedy by the well-known Russian playwright and journalist of the XVIIIth century Denis Fonvisin, published in 1782.　　p. 13

[2] "The Ball" by Evgeni Baratynsky, a friend of Pushkin's.　　p. 21

[3] A story by Bestuzhev-Marlinsky, an active participator in the armed rising of December 14, 1825. Owing to the severity of the tsarist censorship, Pushkin was obliged to omit the name of the author. By quoting his work, however, Pushkin tacitly lets the reader infer his own Decembrist sympathies.　　p. 21

[4] Denis Davydov, poet and writer on military subjects, was a friend of Pushkin's. In 1812 he led a partisan detachment which, aided by volunteers from the peasantry, waged a heroic struggle against the French invaders. Burtsov, a participator in the Patriotic War of 1812, is frequently mentioned in the poems of Denis Davydov.　　p. 27

[5] The first edition continues:
At last I came to the decision to go to bed as early as possible, and dine as late as possible; in this way I shortened the evening and added to the day, and considered that this was the best thing I could do.　　p. 30

[6] A Russian general. In 1820 he was one of the leaders of a secret revolutionary society for the liberation of Greece from the Turkish

invaders. On June 29, 1821, Ipsilanti's detachment was defeated by Turkish troops at the village of Skulyani, on the river Prut.

[7] From "Svetlana," a ballad by the Russian poet and translator Vasili Zhukovsky (1783-1852).   p. 39

[8] *Wit Works Woe*, the famous comedy by the XIX-century Russian dramatist and diplomat Alexander Griboyedov. This play, written by Pushkin's contemporary, belongs, like Pushkin's own revolutionary poems, to the outstanding productions of the Decembrist epoch.   p. 49

[9] "The Waterfall," an ode by the distinguished Russian XVIII-century poet Gavriil Derzhavin.   p. 57

[10] The allusion is to the main character in a novel by Alexei Perovsky, a XIX-century author whose pen-name was Antoni Pogorelsky.   p. 60

[11] Pyotr Vyazemsky, XIX-century poet.   p. 69

[12] Terentyich, a domestic serf in the poem "Caricature," by a XVIII-century Russian poet Ivan Dmitriev.   p. 82

[13] "Sweetheart," a poem by the Russian XVIII-century poet Ippolit Bogdanovich.   p. 87

[14] A character in Fonvisin's comedy *The Dunce*; a typical landowner and serf-holder, boorish and ignorant.   p. 108

Printed in the Union of Soviet Socialist Republics